I0671790

LOVE
FIRE & ICE

———

V. Marie

Brock Media, LLC
C. CLEARLY BOOKS

Atlanta, Georgia

Love Fire & Ice

Copyright © 2013 by V. Marie

Published by C. CLEARLY BOOKS a subsidiary of Brock Media, LLC.

All rights reserved. No part of this book may be used or reproduced by any means, graphic, electronic, or mechanical, including photocopying, recording, taping or by any information storage retrieval system without the written permission of the publisher except in the case of brief quotations embodied in critical articles and reviews.

ISBN 978-0-9889446-4-0

Printed in the United States of America
All rights reserved.

Cover image: istockphoto.com

This is a work of fiction. Any references to real people, places, events, establishments, organizations, products, incidents, or dialogue in this novel either is the products of the author's imagination or used fictitiously.

I dedicate this book
to the love of my life.

Chapters

ne

In the fall, Las Vegas had nearly perfect weather, today was no exception. Many of the visitors to Sin City either overdress or underdress this time of year. Vanity thought for today's meeting she would wear her kick-ass suit that always covered her unshapely figure. As much as she tried to create curves in the right places through diet and exercise, she always failed in the breast and stomach department. Vanity really believed her breasts and stomach were huge and when she undressed, every other part of her body fell in the same category. Her husband, Winston, for whatever reason would never say one way or another if she was fat; but even if he did not say it, she felt like it.

Vanity's closet held clothes for months of wearing, outfits that spanned decades and she often tried on several before deciding on the right one. The house she designed over ten years ago, she purposely created a space especially for her things. She affectionately referred to this area as the "V spot" the area, the space that contained all her "stuff". Stuff or better yet, memories trapped within "things" she had accumulated over twenty years. Whenever Winston would come into the V spot, his first words would always be "when are you going to throw some of this stuff out?" No matter what the situation, his first thoughts of Vanity's things, memories, stuff was junk. Vanity had never explained, never wanted to take the time to define her possessions to Winston, and would smile to herself because she had something for herself that no other person in the world could share in.

Women in business are a magnet for handbags, shoes, and clothes. She always thought if a woman was not a collector of one of the three, you might want to check the "pedigree" just to make sure she was truly a woman. For Vanity, shopping was not just for the sake of shopping. Shopping was a form of therapy, what some call an addiction. An addiction she would take to her grave.

Today, she was a little unsure about the kick-ass suit she picked out. For some reason it didn't make her look so hot anymore. The reality of turning forty in a few weeks played badly on her ego, and hampered her self-esteem. She was looking at herself at all angles in her wall mirror and, then at that moment, it hit her; she was aging and it was starting to show. She broke into a sweat, which had been happening a lot lately. She immediately stripped from the suit and rushed to get a towel to blot and fan before her hair frizzed up. She did not think it was time for menopause but it sure as hell felt like it.

After nearly fifteen minutes, she was dressed again in another suit she felt hid her flaws, applied her makeup, and put her naturally thick and curly locks in a ponytail. Vanity was ready for the office. Today she had a presentation for potential business of sizeable nature. It was a new project from a few executives out of Denver. Her partner, Nicole, had initially taken on this deal but she was out on maternity leave. Their assistant, Michelle, worked around the clock to get details in order for the meeting so all Vanity had to do was present it.

After fifteen years, Vanity saw all new deals as a walk in the park, but for some reason, internally, she felt different about this one, but she attributed this feeling to her pending fortieth.

Before leaving for the office, she went to down to the kitchen for coffee and to her in-home office to write her daughter, Christina, an email and create her daily to do list. When she made it down, she realized her husband had already left for the office.

Winston, taught at the local university and was usually gone by the time she made her way down for coffee, today was no exception. She would start her day alone. They lived in the suburbs of the city and the view of the mountains was her daily dose of tranquility. The kitchen had a view that overlooked the mountains to the east and she had the deck built so that she could step outside on any morning and watch the sunrise from behind the mountains. On the way to the den, she checked her phone and realized her assistant called. It must have been during that last hot flash, she thought.

"Hi, Mrs. Davis, it's Michelle. I was calling to let you know that Mr. McKnight had requested to meet a little later due to inclement weather leaving out of Denver. Your schedule is open so I told him that would be fine. See you when you get in." Vanity deleted the message and realized she was blessed with some extra time before heading to the office. The morning greeting to her daughter was brief as it was on most mornings and she finished her list of things to do.

On the way to the office her phone rang, it was Nicole. "Good morning," she said.

"Hi, Van. I was calling to see if you have everything you need for the meeting this morning," Cole said.

"Oh yea, Michelle and I have everything under control and the McKnight firm called to push the meeting back because of weather problems leaving Denver," Vanity told her.

"Okay. I am so delirious some mornings because

I'm not getting enough sleep," Nicole said.

"I'm sure! But girl, remember the golden rule."

"What golden rule is that exactly? Nicole asked with a laugh.

"You better be sleeping when the baby is sleeping. That's the golden rule," Vanity said with an advising motherly laugh.

"Well that's what I try to do, but you know how it is. There are a million and one things that need to be done while the baby is sleeping," Nicole replied.

"Get your rest and I'll tell you about the meeting this afternoon," Vanity said in a reassuring voice.

They hung up and Vanity could not help but smile as she thought about her friend and partner. From the day, Cole told her she was pregnant, Vanity always said she was crazy to be starting at forty. Nicole and her husband had been trying for a long time and finally they got pregnant. Vanity thought her friend's biological clock had done all its ticking but at thirty-nine, she finally conceived. Although she was happy for her friend, she was worried that at her age things would be harder for her to deal with as a new mother.

When Vanity arrived at the office, she realized that she still had some time to check voicemail and email. Winston had called and left a message that he would be home late; which was nothing new. They both had started doing that lately to avoid being bothered with each other. She never asked what he did at school so late; she had become accustomed to the space, and at this stage, didn't really care anymore. Vanity gained freedom to explore and create, dive into her career without feeling that she was neglecting him.

In college, when Winston and Vanity met she thought they had enough in common to keep their marriage spicy for years. They used to do many things together, but togetherness began to fade into their separate lives. Now that they had both reached their late thirties, she often felt that neither of them was interested in the other. They lived together with their mundane routines and their sexless lifestyle became more like roommates than husband and wife or even friends. Sex had fizzled out for them some time ago and work took the forefront. Vanity had come to realize that her life was passing her by and that she was not happy with the man she chose to spend the rest of her life with. She felt this way for some time and knew she needed and wanted more.

"Good morning, Michelle," Vanity said as she walked past the receptionist's desk to her office. Michelle was on the phone and she waved. Vanity planned to get a few things done so she could be ready for the meeting when the McKnight Firm arrived. As expected, when she got to her desk a copy of the presentation for the meeting was laying out as instructed. Michelle was a diligent assistant, almost anticipatory of Vanity and Nicole's work needs. Vanity reviewed the final version of the presentation, and she was ready to make the pitch and close this deal.

When Vanity started going through her email, she saw that Christina had responded and said that she would be home for Vanity's birthday. She always anticipated her daughter's visits home, and it made her smile to know that Christina would be home to help her bring in the big 4-0. At the knock on her door, she looked up to see Michelle.

"Yes?" she asked.

"Mr. Dexter McKnight is here. Would you like me to escort him to the conference room?" Michelle asked.

"Did you say Dexter McKnight?"

"Yes, Mr. McKnight of McKnight Enterprises. Is there something wrong?" Michelle asked.

"Uh, no, the name rang a bell, but I'm sure it's someone else. I know a Dexter McKnight from Denver, that's all," Vanity said in a nonchalant manner, dismissing the thought from her mind.

"Okay," Michelle said puzzled.

Michelle escorted McKnight to the conference room and came back to Vanity's office to let her know that everything was ready to go.

"Thank you, Michelle," Vanity said and gathered her things, paused for a moment to breathe, and headed to the conference room.

She felt a slight sweat coming on but she did not know why. She was never nervous before a presentation. Besides, this couldn't be *the* Dexter McKnight from high school. Before getting to the conference room, she had to stop by the restroom to blot, fan and check her makeup. No matter who this person was, she had to calm her nerves before entering the conference room, she couldn't appear flushed, but poised and in control. The fanning was working and she calmed down within a minute or two.

When she went into the conference room and their eyes met, her heart nearly stopped. It *was* Dexter McKnight from high school. She immediately took an assessment and realized that he was different; obviously aging just as she had, but his style and presence was unlike the Dexter she knew back in the day. His suit and tie were definitely Italian and his hands, nicely manicured and to top off his look; his physique was in tiptop shape. Over the past twenty years, she had rarely visited home and had never run into Dexter. This person sitting in her conference room was not the person she remembered from high school; age had definitely been good to him. Not only had he made a name for himself to afford *her* business, but also he was damn good looking.

"Dexter?"

"Vanity Rodriquez?" He stood to greet her.

"Yes. Well, it's Vanity Davis now," she said extending a hand but he grabbed her for a hug instead.

"Well how are you?" Dexter asked in a genuine curious tone of voice.

"I am doing very well. I see you are here to do some big business. Of course, I didn't know it was you or *your* firm. This is my partners deal; I'm sitting in for her." Vanity said.

"Oh yea, I was expecting to meet Nicole Daniels today, right?"

"Yes, that is correct. She's out on family leave so I stepped in."

Dexter, smiling like a kid in a candy shop said, "I had no idea this was your firm since you've changed your name."

"Well after college, I left Colorado for a faster paced climate and been in business with Nicole for fifteen years."

"Wow. You're obviously doing something right," said Dexter, "This is a very popular firm and came highly recommended."

Vanity watched every nuance of his manner, right down to how he sat down at the conference table. She thought to herself that this Dexter is secure, comfortable in his skin, in control.

Vanity said, "Well, thank you and I don't want to take too much of your time so shall we get started?"

She wanted to wrap up the small talk realizing that she started to check him out and needed to get her focus back on the task. Vanity said to herself, "Make the deal and avoid a hot flash."

"Sure," he said turning his attention to the projector screen.

She turned toward the screen to start the presentation and she felt like he was watching her. She became immediately self-conscious and started thinking about the kick-ass suit she picked out that probably made her look fat. When she turned to look at him and saw his eyes on the presentation, she tried to relax and calm down. Nevertheless, it was too late; she felt the hair on her neck curl up. Within fifteen minutes, she was taking off her jacket; she felt the heat building and couldn't take it anymore.

"Are you okay?" Dexter asked.

"Is it a little warm in here to you?" Vanity replied as she fanned with a page from the presentation.

"No. Are you coming down with a cold or something? You look a little flushed, are you feeling okay?"

Little did he know that at the early age of thirty-nine her hormones were out of whack and that she was just going through a hot flash.

"Can I step out for a second? I'm fine. I just need a minute. I apologize." She grabbed her blazer and phone from the conference table and rushed to the restroom.

Vanity called Michelle and asked for a towel from her office powder room. Michelle came frantically to the restroom to make sure she was okay.

"What's wrong?" Michelle asked.

"A hot flash. Can you grab my makeup bag from my purse?" Vanity asked.

Michelle went to her office and returned with the makeup bag. Vanity also asked Michelle to go to the conference room and check on Dexter.

Vanity told Michelle, "Make sure he has fresh water and give him a little small talk for me. I'll be right out."

She washed her face in the restroom basin to freshen up. She had to hurry through this presentation because her nerves, for whatever reason, were all out of sorts or was it this man?

"Shit, pull it together girl, this is just another damn deal!" Vanity spoke aloud. Quickly she was firmly back in control, strolled into the conference room, and resumed right from where she left off without as much as a blink of an eye.

After another hour, the presentation concluded. Dexter said he would advise his partners to seek VanCole Marketing services for their new venture in Vegas. Nicole had developed a very attractive deal that would give them exactly what they needed to expand and receive striking returns on investment. If McKnight decided to accept their terms, it would be the beginning of a long-term relationship with McKnight Enterprises and VanCole Marketing.

"Mrs. Davis," Dexter said with a smirk and professional voice, "I expect to get this information back to my partners and will get back to you within a few days. Is that okay?" he asked.

"Of course, again, I apologize about earlier. It must be the weather getting to me."

They both started gathering their things and there was an odd silence in the room. She felt like saying something but could not get it out. Dexter broke the silence.

"You know, I am here until tomorrow. I would really like to catch up with you over dinner. Are you free?" Dexter asked.

"As a matter of fact, I am. My husband will be working late and I would have gone out anyway. Are you staying on the strip?"

"I am staying at the Imagination. How about six? I have a few conference calls and would like to catch an hour or two of sleep."

"Sounds good, I'll meet you in the restaurant at six." In the most business professional manner, Vanity extended her hand for a firm shake as Dexter was leaving the room.

****

Vanity had two other presentations for the day, and because of her earlier blast from the past, she could not keep her attention on the business deals in front of her. She managed to get through them but at the oddest moments, she found herself drifting off, wondering about Dexter, who he had become. At the wrap up with her last client, she checked her watch and it was nearly five-thirty. Thankfully, they had an office near the strip and the Imagination was only blocks away. She could be in the parking lot and headed into the hotel within minutes. By doing business with so many of the hotels and casinos in Vegas, there were unlimited benefits. She could stay at many of the major hotels and eat on an open tab. Vanity found benefits like these to be an obvious advantage, especially when she could pass them on to some of her better paying clients for strong repeat business.

"Ahh, Mrs. Davis, so nice to see you. Are you meeting or dining with us this evening?" the attendant asked.

"Good evening Stan, I am dining so can you please park me close?" she requested. Vanity had purchased her Maserati less than a year ago and the hotel loved to park her exotic wheels near the front.

"Yes, ma'am. Have a great time," Stan escorted her from the car.

Inside the hotel, as the tourists looked around, she whizzed by trying to avoid being late. She was hoping that Dexter was not waiting too long. She really did not have the chance to freshen up, but since this was old friends catching up, she should be okay, she thought. When she arrived at the restaurant area, he was there waiting, as she suspected. He had clearly changed his attire from his business suit to a buttoned down shirt with jeans and hard bottom shoes. Dexter smiled as Vanity approached.

"Hi, Vanity," he said.

"Hi, Dex," she said then quickly realized her greeting was less than formal.

"Damn, did I just call him Dex? Ok just move forward with it, don't gloss over a name, smile and act relaxed," she thought to herself.

Dexter also greeted her with a hug with a kiss on the cheek just before he nodded to the host to seat them. He had arranged for special seating, with no waiting and like most nights, dining in the Imagination was crowded.

Although Vanity had dined at this restaurant many times for meetings, apparently there were other sections for privacy and special occasions off the beaten path that she didn't know about.

"I never knew there was private dining," Vanity said in a low tone, but loud enough for Dexter to hear.

"Yea, I asked for something away from the crowd. I wanted us to have some time to catch up without being rushed by the tourist crowd."

"Hmm, good idea. You know how to use your resources, I like that in a client," Vanity said with a girlish smile.

Seating Vanity at the table first seemed to be a natural motion for Dexter; trained, experienced in the art of seating a woman as he pulled out her chair. This simple act gained him high honors in Vanity's already growing esteem. When he sat across from her the waiter immediately came over to their table and placed the napkins on their laps. He took their drink orders of which, Vanity was having a glass of Chateau Brion white, in an attempt to keep it light. In stark contrast, Dexter ordered Beefeater Gin with a splash of ginger ale and slice of lime. The waiter smiled at his choice and proceeded to give them the evening specials.

No sooner than the waiter walked away, Dexter started with the questions.

"So who did you marry?" He asked.

"His name is Winston Davis. He's from Nevada. We actually met while I was in college and I was vacationing in Vegas. He was born and raised here and when I graduated from college, I decided to move to Vegas. We've been married for eighteen years."

Vanity said this as if it was merely a happening and not a joyous event or time in her life and Dexter noticed.

"Do you have children?" Dexter asked.

"I have a daughter. She's a freshman at Yale," Vanity replied.

"Nice college.   What's she studying?" Dexter seemed to be very interested, as he peered into Vanity's eyes.

"Marketing.   She's looking to take over the firm someday."

Vanity started to notice he was watching her a little seductively, or was it the wine and her imagination. Either way, she felt him looking at her a little too much.

"I see gin is your drink of choice tonight, Mr. McKnight," she said trying to get used to talking to him like a client, since that is what he was.

With a slight laugh and very seductive smile, "I am drinking gin for medicinal purposes. It keeps my mind sharper than Kettle One, and much less of a headache if I have one too many. Would you care to join me for a glass?" He asked with a wink to follow.

What the hell was that, Vanity thought. Was he flirting? She rubbed her hair to make sure it was still intact and tried to keep her nerves in check without him noticing. She didn't remember Dexter being this damn sexy. His voice was seductive and raspy, his skin was smooth and his smile was to die for. His demeanor was cool and he had a swag that would turn any woman on, especially her.

"What is up with you these days? How long have you been in business?" Vanity totally ignored his question and tried to recompose herself.

"Let's see...my cousin and a few partners of mine started a chain of restaurants about seven years ago and have since grown and now we want to expand," he explained.

"Really? Is it anyone from Mary Haven High?"

"Actually, a couple you may know. I'm sure we will do business with you, now that I know who I'm investing in. You'll see them soon," he finished and he winked again.

What was up with that, she thought, "I'm not dreaming, he winked again. This man could not honestly find me attractive. He hasn't seen me in over twenty years." Vanity became a little self-conscious; as she thought about the fifty pounds, she put on since high school, and no longer looked like arm candy, or a Vegas hottie. Although money and cosmetics have made her look younger in some places, the weight gain was a whole other story and she did not have the courage to get surgery. Their next round of drinks came and that glass of wine barely got a chance to touch the table before it hit the back of Vanity's throat, much to Dexter's surprise.

Vanity proudly exclaimed, "I'll take that gin now, I guess I was just a little thirsty."

Her look was more playful and she was starting to relax. It was the kind of look that made Dexter grin, as he ushered the waiter to return.

They spent the next two hours talking about their marriages and he told her about his three kids. They had many things in common, both married and barely hanging on, nearly twenty years, unhappy. As the conversation loosened, the waiter kept the rounds coming.

Between the flirtatious looks and winks all night, she figured there was something about her he liked; she just didn't know what. She was trying to stay reserved but after her fifth or sixth drink, it was hard not to return the gestures.

Neither of them had really eaten the meal they ordered, they did so much talking and laughing the time seemed to run away. They had enjoyed each other's company going on three hours. Getting drunk was not typical for Vanity at this age and it was not her intention to get drunk, but it would not be the first time it happened on a work night. Although when she did, she knew better than to drive home. She would check into a hotel.

"Are you going to be okay driving home?" Dexter asked as he reached for her hand across the table.

"Ah, I don't think so. I've stayed at this property often on nights like this."

"What will your husband think?" Dexter questioned.

"Speaking of which, I need to call him. He will wonder but I'll just tell him I ran into an old friend and stayed out for drinks. That does happen often since we *are* in Vegas," she slurred.

Vanity dug her phone out of her bag and called. It was nearly nine and there was no answer at home or his cell phone so she left a message. She was enjoying Dexter's company, not reaching Winston on the phone did not bother her one bit. Vanity was always busy with work these days, and had no real down time, so this felt good. She and Winston very seldom did anything spectacular and this was exciting to her.

"I need to call and get a room and have the valet park my car in the lot," Vanity said after leaving the message.

She dialed the hotel and made the arrangements while Dexter sat across the table from her just watching. She wondered what was going through his mind at that moment. Was he thinking nasty thoughts? Did he find her attractive? What? Vanity, was finally calm, relaxed and felt very comfortable, was able to look at him without feeling nervous.

Dexter softly said, "Since you're staying, would you like to walk off some of that alcohol? It's been a while since I've walked the Vegas strip."

"You know, that would be nice," Vanity replied.

He paid the check and they walked out of the hotel onto the strip. Dexter walked a little closer then she would have expected but it was cool. The water show was just starting and they stopped to see flashing lights and splashing water.

The fall night air was getting a little chilly so Vanity grabbed her own arms to warm up. When Dexter noticed, he stood behind her and wrapped his arms around her in a bear hug and instantly, she warmed up. She was frantically hoping it was a false alarm and that she would not start sweating. Thankfully, she did not get too warm but just the right temperature to make her fall back into his chest. She could feel every muscle in his frame. He obviously had no reservations about rubbing on her body trying to warm her. In the one moment that she should be self-conscious about her rolls, she let his hands wander. Under the night-lights of the city, no one cared to watch them, she didn't care if they did, and she fell into the moment. His lips made their way to her neck and he inhaled the scent from her skin before he kissed it. His juicy lips were soft and her neck enjoyed every minute of it. Her ear was next. Around her pink diamond stud, he kissed her ear bringing instant pleasure to somewhere deep in her. By now, far more than her neck and ears were wet from his lips. The light show was going on in front of them and when the music and splashing water finally stopped, she snapped out of the moment like the flip of a light switch.

"Dexter, what are we doing?"

"I don't want you to do anything but stand here and allow my lips the pleasure of tasting your sweet skin," he let out a moan as he kissed her neck once again.

His moan sent a shiver straight to her pussy. She tried to remain calm but she could not stay still anymore. He not only had her turned on, but on full blast. Vanity felt as if she was twenty-one again, but they were still standing in public and she had started noticing people watching them. She was no longer in the moment.

"Dexter, we have to move along," she freed herself from his bear hug and turned to face him.

"I'm sorry Vanity. It's just that you have no idea how much I needed that," he said.

"You? Hell, I needed it. I just think if we don't stop we'll become a little too obvious out here."

"You're right. I'm sorry. Let's move on."

He grabbed her hand and put it through his arm as a man takes his bride to be. He was pulling her closer to him. He had no idea how good it felt to her. Vanity wanted to hurry to her room; she wanted to pleasure herself to the thought of his lips, his touch. Dexter had her temperature rising every time he touched her. They made it down to a few more sights on the strip before they turned back toward the Imagination.

"So, you are a sin city girl now?" he said jokingly.

"Well, if that's what you want to call it but I don't make it a habit of meeting up with men and letting them kiss all over me if that's what you mean."

"Naa, I didn't say that and didn't mean to imply that," he replied.

"Regardless of how unhappy I am in my marriage, I have never done anything like this before," Vanity said in a matter of fact tone.

"What have you done? You haven't done anything," he said with a measure of reassurance.

"You know...this. Walking down the romantic strip of Las Vegas and kissing in front of the water show. This!" Vanity said.

"Oh. You didn't do anything. That was all me!" he said trying to convince her that she was innocent.

"See, it's not that *you* didn't do it. *I* allowed it. I enjoyed it. I wanted you to keep going," Vanity admitted.

"Oh, you shouldn't have told me that," he grabbed her closer, tickling her side.

"Oh no! I don't think so!" She playfully tried to release her arm from his grasp.

They both laughed and he teased her all the way back to the hotel. She was hoping that they could just get there and part ways. Spending more time with him would be a bad idea. She felt like she had to make up some excuse to go up to her room without him.

"Vanity, I'll walk you up to your room to make sure you get in okay. Do you need to get your key?"

"Oh, shit," Vanity, thought. He was slick. He was going to try that famous movie scene. Get to the door and kiss her then push the door open and next thing you know they'll be having hot passionate sex. Vanity thought the visual was exciting, but she could not let that happen.

"Dexter, thanks but I think I can manage on my own," she answered hoping he caught the hint.

He did accompany her to the desk to get her key but then she stopped at the gift shop to get a ginger ale and some aspirin just in case she woke up with a hangover. She had to be at the office on time in the morning for a few meetings and didn't want to take any chances. She had to get some sleep. It was nearly eleven and she was typically in bed by then.

After she stopped at the gift shop, they stopped by the elevators to say their goodbyes.

"Well, Van, it was so nice to see you. I look forward to seeing more of you," Dexter said.

"Dexter, what do you actually mean by that?" Vanity asked.

"I mean that it's been a very pleasant surprise to see you. I had no idea that you were here and it's been a long twenty years, and I must say, you still look good." She noticed his teeth, bright and white, as he smiled the ending words.

He finally said it "you still look good". He actually thought she was attractive. She could not believe it. This man, even at thirty-nine could get a twenty something year old chick and he was looking at her.

Dexter said, "Back in high school, I don't think we ever really got a chance to talk like that. You had your friends and I had mine. I think we just overlooked each other back then, at least I know you overlooked me. So, seeing you all grown up and the way I'm feeling, is new for me, too. I have not been with any other woman other than my wife and tonight, I am craving you."

"I have to admit, when I saw you in my office today, I almost lost my mind. Aging is not always good to people but maturity is sexy as hell on you," Vanity responded.

"Damn girl, you can't say that shit and leave me standing in this lobby. Are you sure I can't walk you up?"

"If I let you walk me up. That's as far as we go," she smiled.

"Scouts honor," Dexter smiled back.

They waited for the elevator in silence and when they got inside, she pressed the P for the Penthouse floor.

"They give you preferential treatment don't they?"

"Yea, the Imagination is one of our major clients. The perks are nice. It's also nice because without a penthouse key, you cannot access my floor," she said and winked at him. "I'm under lock and key. I can tell you're trouble."

Dexter laughed and said, "I am an innocent bystander. If you didn't turn me on, none of this would be happening."

When the elevator stopped, they got out and headed toward her room. She was hoping that he kept his cool because if he touched her like he did earlier, she did not know if she could stop him. At her door, she stopped and faced him.

"Dexter, it was such a pleasure seeing you, too. It was indeed a surprise and outside of business, I hope we can stay in touch."

"Vanity, you have made me laugh and smile a lot tonight and it's been a while since I did that, thank you.

I want to kiss you goodnight..." he paused, grabbed her by the neck, and brought her to his lips.

She matched his kiss in pleasure and teasing. His hands found their way to the slope of her ass and then to her breast. She hoped the hotel cameras were not catching all of this. He went to her neck and this time she got a whiff of his intoxicating cologne. She still had her key in her hand, as she wiggled her way around to open the door to the room. She turned back to look at Dexter in the eyes and he waited until she stepped aside to allow him in. Once he stepped beyond the threshold, he scooped her up, took her in his arms, and brought her into the sitting room of the suite.

Dexter playfully said to Vanity "I was never a scout," as he laid her on the sofa and proceeded to remove her pumps. He took each leg in his hand and massaged it from thigh to toes. Her body was craving his lips to touch it. With each wet kiss, her clitoris wondered what his lips, his tongue, slow and long felt like. She imagined it fast, harder, swift, to a tingle burn. She wanted him to taste her, and make her moan into a scream.

It was coming and her body was responding to each touch and her vivid imagination. Vanity's senses became inflamed with desire, hot with lust and passion; her pussy throbbed, not like when she made it cum, better. Before she knew it her eyes had closed, head laid back on the chase, relaxed with expectation. All she could think about was how good it felt to have someone give her body the attention it needed for the longest time.

"Van," he whispered.

"Yes?" her eyes still closed.

"Ever since I can remember, I've wanted to have this moment with you."

"What?"

"Yea, you never knew but I have wanted you for a long time."

He parted her thick thighs with kisses that made her tingle as she became wetter and nerve endings seemed to throb in rhythm. "Damn," she thought. Her body relaxed, tried to prepare itself for what was about to happen. There are times when you want something so bad that you don't always know what you have is not good enough anymore, and then something new comes along and surprises you. That was Dexter.

When his lips touched and he sucked on her clit, her body melted, her juice flowed like water all over. He had patience with her. Teased and played with her clit, bringing it to near explosion three or four times it seemed. Her hand stayed to her side, as she had no reason to guide him along; he knew exactly what he was doing. He wanted her to reach peeks and then gently slide to valleys making her eventual climax massive, multiple and intense. His tongue was strong and lips soft, faster and with more pressure, in that one spot, "Shit," in a voice she did not recognize as her own. She felt the tip of his chin on her lips as his tongue gave her clit pleasure. Vanity's mind could not process this intense type of pleasure; it was unreal to her mind and body. His lips began a grinding motion on the meat of her pussy. "Damn," that voice again. Her moans and movement increased as her pelvis gave way to his pleasing tongue dance. Dexter felt the tension building in her body. He felt her juice flowing quicker as his chin became wetter. She grabbed his head and her thighs clamped down as she screamed the letter O like a Negro spiritual. Vanity came in an unfamiliar way. It was the type of orgasm that she had read about. The kind she tried to achieve on her own late at night in the dark of her room, but to no avail. Vanity, in thirty-nine years of life had her very first multiple orgasm. Dexter came up to her, kissed her lips.

"Was that all right?" he whispered.

"All right? That was..." she was interrupted by the sound of her phone ringing across the room where she dropped it when they came in. "Shit. It's probably Winston. I'd better get it."

Dexter was between her legs and she could not move until he did. He stood up and went to get her purse.

"Hello," she said groggily.

"Yes, I'm at the Imagination. I'll be home after work tomorrow. Yes, friends from home…yes, a little too much, uh huh, okay," she said in a hurrying voice. Winston apparently was just getting in after listening to her message. She hung up the phone and brought her attention back to Dexter.

"Now, what were you saying?" he asked.

"It was amazing and I never knew you had a thing for me," Vanity replied.

"There are a lot of things you probably don't know," Dexter responded.

"Well, I guess I'm about to learn." Vanity said as she smiled and then buried her face in the palms of her hands, slightly embarrassed, yet very turned on by the course of events.

"This is true and I do want to apologize for violating my scouts honor." Dexter joked, and Vanity again noticed how his grin seemed so seductively sexy, especially in this moonlit room.

"Oh, it's okay," she said with a laugh, "I knew you weren't a scout, and I wanted you too from the moment

I stepped into that conference room but didn't want to admit it," Vanity said.

"Oh, really? We don't have to stop here." Dexter enthusiastically responded.

"Dex, we're married."

Vanity tried to bring some form of control back to the banter between them, but she wanted to feel his dick inside of her.

"Please, don't remind me," Dexter said.

"What do you mean don't remind you? What's going on?" Vanity wanted to know more, she needed to understand the common ground that paralleled their lives.

"I really don't want to talk about it," Dexter responded as he went to the window to look out onto the bright lights on the strip.

"Oh ok, but that's not a good answer for me," Vanity started, "I am not going to allow all of this to happen and you leave to go back to Denver and not know what's up with your situation back home. Tell me what's up," Vanity finished.

"I guess I'm just not happy anymore. It's taken a long time to realize it, but after twenty years you'd think I'd still be madly in love or settled into my marriage and life, but I'm not." Dexter turned with his back now to the panoramic window and the moonlight as his backdrop.

"I know what you mean but how did we get here, like this?" Vanity responded sympathetically.

"I told you Van, this is something that I thought about. I had heard you moved on and got married. I hadn't seen you in so many years, so I tucked away my feelings about you." Dexter was sincere, it made Vanity wonder what her life what be like today if she had been open to giving him a chance, if he would have approached her so many years earlier.

"I guess I did leave home and never really came back," Vanity slowly responded.

"Yea, I think I may have seen you a few times before you graduated from college but that's about it," Dexter said.

"What a day," she said finally.

"Yea, what a day. Is that my cue to make my way to my room?"

"Actually, I was hoping you'd stay."

They stood up and went over to the bedroom in the suite. It was fully equipped with linen, robes and a large built in bar with drinks and snacks. Vanity picked up the remote and pressed the button to close the curtains.

"I need to shower; it's been a long day. Will you be okay? Do you need room service or anything?" she said pulling the scrunchie from her hair and shuffled her locks to loosen them up.

"No, I think I'm good. I'll catch a little ESPN," Dexter said.

Vanity smiled and thought that all men were the same when it came to sports. The best day they had could always end with catching up on sports.

The luxurious bathroom was an escape for Vanity to recompose herself. Vanity looked at herself in the mirror. She didn't want to jump into bed with a man she had not seen in twenty years. It was bad enough she allowed him to take her there. What was she thinking? This was a very bad idea. Vanity stepped into the shower and the water smacked against her face like a reality check. Her stomach flip-flopped. She cheated on her husband, she despised cheaters, and here she became one of them, in 30 seconds. She wasn't good with lying and this secret, she knew, would eat her alive. That feeling of alcohol disagreeing with an empty stomach came over her and she was dry heaving in the shower.

Dexter overheard the noise, "Are you okay?"

"Yeah, too many drinks," she lied.

"Do you want that ginger ale?"

"Yea, in a minute," she replied.

Vanity felt sick to her stomach for what she had done. How could they be business associates under these conditions? Vanity explored her mind to place the blame any and everywhere, but her own doorstep. She said to herself, "That damn Nicole, it's all her fault. If she had not been on maternity leave none of this would have happened."

"Oh, shit!" she said. Vanity just remembered that she did not call Nicole about the meeting. She was probably thinking it went okay or she would have called by now, but how the hell would Vanity include this in the conversation.

"Van, your phone is ringing. It says, Cole on it," Dexter called out.

"Damn. Speak of the devil," she said. She and Cole had a quasi-physic connection for years, every time one thought about the other; the other would call or appear.

She hit the shower release and grabbed a robe from the hook. Before she could reach the phone, it had stopped.

Vanity immediately called her back, "Hey, Cole."

"Hey yourself! Where the hell have you been? Michelle said you went to a meeting and that was the last she heard from you. Why didn't you call me? How did the deal go?"

"Calm down. The meeting went great and Mr. McKnight is seriously interested."

Dexter turned as he heard those words and came over toward her as she tried to hurry and tie the robe.

"Oh, okay. I hope that means we got the deal. Where are you now?"

"I'm at the Imagination. I had dinner this evening with an old friend from high school, so I didn't want to drive home." Dexter stood behind her, untying the robe to expose her naked body.

"The Imagination? Penthouse?"

"You know it. Hey, I have to go. You interrupted my steamy shower. I'll catch up with you in the morning. Kiss my niece for me." Vanity ended the conversation quickly, as her body warmed to Dexter's touch.

"Okay. You know I'll be up, so call me."

"Will do," Vanity responded and hung up, as the moisture between her thighs had not come from the shower, but from the man pressed firmly against her.

Dexter made his way into her robe and managed to pull the tie out to keep her from retying it. His hands wanted to explore her body more but he could feel her hesitation.

"Are you okay with this?" he asked.

"Actually, no. I don't know what I was thinking to let things get this far and asking you to stay."

With those words, he gave her back the tie to the robe and she closed off her body from his view. It was the first awkward moment of the entire day.

She was hoping that he didn't get offended, as she really did want to fuck his socks off, but she knew that it would only lead to more, and that would lead to nowhere. She did not love him, but she was infatuated. They both had spouses and lives that would be a total mess if things got out of hand. He gathered his things and started making his way to the door. Dexter looked back and winked at her one last time before he turned and left. Vanity listened to the door close and he was gone.

Two

For the next week all Vanity could think about was Dexter. She made it her business to do some extra work at the office just to stay away from home. The firm remained busy and between new clients and associates, there was always something to do. Winston had become accustomed to her coming home late or not at all on some nights. Vanity thought he probably felt the same way she did, he just would not admit it. Their marriage was pretty much a lifestyle they lived and she felt like on the inside they both dreaded it. She hoped one day he would come home and say he was tired of the marriage and they quietly parted ways but in reality, Winston was not that type of man and she did not see him deciding to leave spontaneously.

The McKnight firm agreed to the terms of the deal within the week. This meant more meetings with Dexter to make this partnership work. McKnight representatives planned to be in Vegas within the week to start round tabling development and strategy plans for the project. Vanity dedicated a team of associates to work on the campaign. Their marching orders were simple, "Come up with a presentation, slogan and campaign that looked better than any cola company." Michelle informed Vanity that all of the partners from McKnight would be there, which was a safe thought for Vanity, but also pressure that she would shoulder as she hid the truth of her feelings from her partner, associates and Winston. But why? It was just one night, not even a complete night, but Vanity felt the burn in her stomach for Dexter already, worst of all she now had to hide the truth from herself. Her plan to keep Dexter out of her head hinged on another major deal coming up the same week, if she was lucky, she might not even be around that much to interact with him. At least that was her plan, create distance, and try to forget.

Cole was not due back from maternity leave for another few weeks but she wanted to come in and oversee the final touches on the McKnight plan. Vanity still had not told her about the rendezvous and she did not plan on it. Vanity had to make sure it stayed that way because she did not want anyone to get the wrong idea about this deal. Cole would probably be happy to hear that Vanity was finally excited about something other than work, other than someone else's life, but Vanity was not ready to spill the beans, especially on an affair that she knew would not develop into anything.

In the midst of wrapping up for the day, Vanity happened to check the calendar and realized her birthday was quickly approaching. It fell on the day of the McKnight presentation. She had not planned to do anything big and hoped no one else did either. Vanity planned to have an intimate dinner with Winston and Christina and call it a day. She was not into surprises and everyone knew it.

Dexter did not know her birthday, so his coming into Vegas on her birthday weekend, would be merely coincidence.

Vanity's phone rang, but instead of answering the call, she hit the power button on her flat screen. Vanity didn't care who it was. She was not about to sit back down at her desk; she was hungry and food was all she could think about. As she began to place the cellphone in her purse, a text message scrolled across the screen. The message was simple, and from a Denver area code.

"Hey sweetie," it read.

"Oh hell no! It's Dexter." Vanity flopped back down into the chair contemplating on whether or not to respond and if she did, what would she say back, "hey, sweetie"? This man had been running through her mind since he walked out of her hotel room that night and the last thing she needed was him sending text messages. She typed back, "Who is this?" Hell, it really could have been anybody, but she doubted it.

"It's Dex. How's your day going?"

"It's over. I was just leaving when I saw your message," she typed.

"I miss you," he responded.

"Hmm," she thought, "What now? Is he expecting me to say I miss you too? Shit." She did miss him, to the core of her; she missed his subtle touch, his smile, his wink. Vanity missed the man that she knew she should stay away from. Her mind, her better judgment told her not to admit to that now. Conflicted, she rationalized, reasoned, and mentally debated for a minute, she was trying to create space between them; not bring them closer; but she could not lie to him. Vanity lost the tug of war between her conscience and emotions.

"I miss you, too," she typed.

"My day was rather difficult today. I had to fire two associates for stealing from the business."

"Oh, no." she replied.

"Yea, we had to have them arrested and we'll be filing charges."

"I'm sorry to hear about that. I hear you'll be here next Friday," Vanity typed.

"Yea, my partners and I will be there Thursday evening and will stay for the weekend. They're going to use it as a retreat to prepare for this new venture," he replied.

"Sounds good," she said.

"So, I know your birthday is next weekend. The big 4-0." He typed with a smiley face.

"How do you know that?" She wondered.

Dexter's follow up was well timed, "Our birthday's aren't too far apart you know. Mine was last month. I still remember that from school."

"Well, I'll be having dinner with my family, so nothing big," she replied.

"Nothing big for 40? Why not?" He responded back to her text.

"I have yet to embrace it. I'll probably celebrate 40 when I turn 45," she typed back with a smile on her face.

"LOL," he responded back.

"Hey, I'm headed out and I cannot text with my 5-speed, so I'll talk to you next week."

"Next week?" he questioned.

Vanity thought aloud and typed without hesitating, "How about tomorrow?"

Dexter responded, "I'll be in meetings but I'll make myself available."

In a week, this man had entered her world and turned it upside down. She was feeling him and apparently, he was feeling her. She was trying not to show it, but she wanted to see him and talk to him every day. She knew that she shouldn't, she needed to get him off her mind. "Snap out of it," she thought! She grabbed her purse and headed for the door.

Michelle was already gone for the day. The account managers were still meeting and planning into the late hours as usual. She was not a micro manager and would check in with them on the McKnight deal in the morning. It had to be perfect. She wanted to make sure she impressed him as an executive first because in her mind right now she was, "Dexter's sexy slave". The thought was arousing, erotic, but as quickly as it came, she was able to dismiss it.

VanCole was a respected firm, employed some of the top marketing and sales executives in the country. They recruited from only the best colleges and spent a pretty penny making sure they were the best and more importantly, creative as hell. The client base was primarily real estate developers and hospitality; they all had money to spend. VanCole made a healthy living knowing how to spend other people's money. Every now and then, they would pick up other deals for retail stores or restaurants coming to the Vegas market through referrals. That is how the McKnight Firm became a client. The city was constantly changing and as with many cities, it still had room for growth and change.

***

Thursday seemed to roll around quickly. Dexter and Vanity had sent text messages every day since he initiated the communication. It was two weeks since their initial meeting but for Van, it seemed like forever as memories of his touch, his look, his charm played in her head every day. Often at the most inappropriate times, she would recall her orgasm.

When her phone chirped around 9 am, she knew it was Dexter. He took the first flight to the city and planned to be at his hotel around that time.

"Hey, babe," he said in a text message.

"You made it?" she replied.

"I just sat my bags down. Do you want to have lunch before things get crazy?"

"Sure. Where are you staying?" she asked.

"At the Imagination," he replied.

"Why don't I come over for early brunch? I have a one o'clock and I'd hate to arrive late trying to get back."

"Sure, sounds good," he replied.

"I'll be there shortly." Smiling, her fingers typed the last message with anticipation.

Vanity told Michelle she was heading out for brunch with a potential client just in case anyone was looking for her. She instructed her to take messages and do not send any to her phone unless it was her daughter or Cole. Everyone else could wait until she returned.

When she pulled into the valet section of the hotel, the head valet pleasantly greeted her. "Greetings Mrs. Davis, are you here for a meeting?" Stan asked.

"Yes, so please park her close." She said referring to the canary-sun colored Maserati.

She pulled out her phone as she entered the lobby and texted Dexter to come down. She passed the window at the gift shop and caught a glimpse of herself. Her suit today was a rather good choice. She had gone to the mall earlier in the week to buy a few new suits that fit and accentuated her flaws better. Her hair was doing its natural curly thing and her makeup was flawless as usual.

"I'll be right down." He responded.

As Vanity waited near the bar, she glanced at the local news on television. The weather for the weekend would be beautiful. She loved it when she could be outdoors on her birthday. Vanity recalled spending her birthdays on the strip partying, but this year would be different. A slight smile came to her face because she felt special in a way that she had not felt in some time. With that same thought, there was another; the age thing was starting to have an effect on her social life. She felt herself getting old and did not know how to have fun anymore. Vanity realized that her social life was suffering at the thought of doing nothing for her birthday.

It took about ten minutes before Dexter arrived at the bar. He was in his urban style gear; very relaxed but with that "don't get it twisted, I am still the man" look. He approached her and leaned in for a kiss on the cheek.

"You look nice," he complimented her suit choice.

"Thank you," she started, "you don't look so bad yourself."

Dexter asked Vanity, "Are you ready to eat? It's still early; I hope they still have breakfast."

Vanity responded more nonchalant, "Hmm, ok."

The host came over at nearly the same time as Vanity's response to Dexter and asked them if they were ready. Dexter nodded enthusiastically and the host walked them to a booth near the water fountain.

"So, who came with you to Vegas?" Vanity asked.

"Uh, let's see, Markus, William and his wife Tiffany, her sister Krystal. I have a few other partners, that you may not know, but you'll meet them at some point." Dexter replied.

Vanity, in an inquisitive manner said, "Oh, I didn't know your cousin was in business with you. I have not seen Tiffany in years. I didn't know she and William got married. That must have happened after I left for college."

In a flat tone, Dexter replied, "Yea, they've been married just about as long as I have. They have two children. Tiffany's sister, Krystal is married and has a little girl. Markus, he's still single with no kids, 'ole lucky bastard!"

"Oh, yea? That's surprising since he was the lady's man back in high school," Vanity said in a tone that gave Dexter a quick, but fleeting thought.

Dexter replied, "Yea, well, he's had a few close calls but he's stood clear of the whole marriage and kid thing."

"Marriage thing? You say that like you regret or despise being married."

"I don't despise being married. I just wish I had made a different choice. I was young back then and didn't realize who I was when I got married. Now, a little more mature and much more focused on my dreams, we're very different people," Dexter replied.

"Yea, I know what you mean. I was young and didn't know who I was either, but I am not sure if I had waited that I would have made a better choice. I just know now that I would have preferred to be single instead of wondering all of these years if I made the wrong choice."

Dexter, with a measure of sympathy in his voice said, "I understand."

Quickly, he changed subjects, "Hey, do you want to catch a movie later? The rest of the crew plans to do sightseeing and I'm not up for it, and would much rather be with you."

"Dex, I don't know about that. I mean we are business associates now. How do we explain going out to a public place like that?" She asked.

"Yea, Van, I do understand your position, and your circumstance. I guess I wasn't thinking. Well, we can always watch one up in my room. I have a 42" flat screen on the wall. I'm sure there has to be something we could order."

That idea did sound safer, but she was still skeptical. She did not know what going to some place private would do to her. Would she play it cool or let it all hang out? She thought he was slick, but would play along.

"On one condition," she said.

"Shoot."

"I get to pick the movie." Vanity liked the art of negotiation, but she had no idea that Dexter mastered negotiation himself. She would soon find out.

"Oh, that's it? I can handle that. I thought you were about to tell me to keep my hands to myself. Now, that would have been a tough deal to make."

They both laughed. She did not know if his laugh was for the same reason as hers, but she laughed because he said what she really wanted and knew it was a long shot. They finished breakfast and she told him she had to get back to the office for her meeting. Christina would be flying in from Connecticut that evening, but from her previous conversations, Vanity got the impression that Christina would be hanging with friends, so she probably would not have gotten much time with her anyway. It looked like it was a movie date with Dexter.

****

By the end of her day, all she could think about was being alone with Dexter. He was on her mind constantly and it was starting to affect her work. She spent too much time texting and chatting with him when she should be working. Every chance each of them got, they called each other, sometimes with no real conversation, just a need to hear each other's voice and chat for a few moments. Now that he was only blocks away, she was anxious all day. As Vanity's anxiety continued to build, in the blink of an eye it all came to a crashing halt.

"Mrs. Davis?"

"Yes?"

"I have an emergency call for you on line two."

She picked up the receiver, "Hello, this is Vanity Davis speaking."

"Van, this is Rob. It's Cole. We're at the hospital with the baby. Something's wrong with Raya and she wanted me to tell you to come up here right now."

"Oh, no. I'm on my way!" She hung up the phone, grabbed her purse, and ran toward the elevator. Michelle tried to ask what was going on but she did not stop.

Robert was Nicole's husband and he sounded very frantic on the phone. They had worked so hard to have this baby. Complications this soon after the baby was born was not a good sign.

She tried to call Dexter on her way into the hospital but it went straight to voicemail. She was not too keen on leaving messages so she hung up. When she found out where Cole and Robert were, she had zoned completely out on Dexter and focused on her friends.

Seeing Cole bent over in the hospital chair, holding herself and rocking, Vanity ran to her side. "How are you?" she asked, grabbing Cole in her arms. Cole broke down in uncontrollable tears.

"I don't know," were the only words Cole could get out.

"Okay, it's going to be okay. Raya will be fine." Vanity looked over to Robert who was sitting with his head in his hands.

"Where's the doctor?" Vanity asked.

"They just came out and said Raya has to have emergency surgery and they would tell us more as soon as they figure out what's going on." Cole replied.

"What happened at home, Cole?"

"She just started shaking and I panicked because it looked like she was going into a seizure or something." Cole explained.

"Oh, no." Vanity gasped.

"So, when we got here they took her and started hooking up all of these machines and tubes and whisked her off and now we're just waiting."

For the next hour, they waited for a doctor to come and explain what was going on with Raya. Vanity called the office, advised her staff to conduct the presentation with the McKnight firm as scheduled, and left no further instructions. She received several calls from

Dexter but did not answer any of them. She felt bad leaving him hanging, but she had to focus on comforting her best friend.

From the beginning of the pregnancy, they always talked about how she would finally get to be an Auntie. She could not let any distractions keep her from praying for her goddaughter.

Robert and Cole met shortly after she and Vanity graduated from college. They ran in the same social circle and finally made a connection. They dated for a few years before they got married. They were the perfect couple. Vanity often envied their relationship because they seemed to stay in love even through their tough times. After their first year of trying to get pregnant, and suffering two devastating miscarriages, Cole found out that she had endometriosis, a disorder in the female uterus that can cause infertility, and which made it difficult for Cole to get pregnant and carry Raya full term. Not having any complications carrying or delivering Christina, Vanity could not imagine what Cole must be going through. When Raya was born, it was the best day of all of their lives. Their little angel was finally born and she was beautiful. For such a precious baby to begin her life like this was shocking Vanity to her core, but she had to stay strong, she needed to give reassurance to Cole and Rob that everything would be okay and this troubled time would drift away as a memory.

****

By 2 o'clock that afternoon, the doctor came from behind the closed doors and removed his mask. His approach to Nicole and Robert was calm and controlled, as if he had practiced every form of composure, even how to approach situations of apprehension. Suddenly, for Vanity the room seemed to stand still, air itself left the room as the seconds it took the doctor to approach them seemed like an eternity.

"Mr. & Mrs. Grant, I'm Dr. Lester, I handled the surgery and tried to care for Raya…" the doctor began.

Rob said quickly, "What do you mean tried to care for our child, what do you mean tried to care for my baby?"

"I'm sorry, your child did not make it through surgery, Raya suffered a severe case of pertussis but we need to perform an autopsy to be sure. It's an infection most common in children less than 3 months and it attacks the white blood cells. I'm sorry, we did all we could do," the doctor explained.

Nicole fell into Robert's arms and sobbed louder than Vanity had ever heard anyone. Vanity was transfixed on the doctor in disbelief, she could not move, she felt as though breath itself had left her with no return. The rest of the day was a blur.

Vanity remembered going home and taking a scalding hot shower to release some tension. When Christina came home that evening, Winston told her what happened to Raya, and she did not bother her mother, and gave the space she felt Vanity needed. Vanity could hear Christina as she went to her room, she wished Christina had come in and gotten into bed with her. She wanted to hold her the way a mother holds a newborn baby. She wanted to feel life in her arms, she needed her daughter's presence and to thank God for her precious life. When she did not come in, Vanity turned off the lamp, powered down her phone, and cried softly into sleep.

It had been a long time since she had slept like this, a long time since she had to take sleeping pills to ease the pain her brain seemed to send through her body. Last night was different for Vanity; she was hurt, afraid and angry. Yesterday was supposed to be a good day and yet it ended with her best friend losing her precious baby girl. She could not imagine Cole recovering any time soon from this. Losing a child, she had heard, is something that you never truly get over. She couldn't imagine Nicole trying again. This was probably her last chance to have a child.

Even though she wanted to get more sleep when the alarm went off, her body automatically went vertical. She got up, showered, and went down for coffee. Winston had Friday's off at the college and had already brewed a pot. "Good morning, how are you?" he asked.

"I'm okay," she was short.

"Are you going to the office?" He asked.

"I don't plan on it," she replied.

"I didn't want to bother you last night, but what happened?" Winston genuinely needed to know.

Vanity took Winston through the chain of events from the previous day. She could not get through the story without crying.

"Would you like to go out for breakfast?" Winston asked changing the subject as he saw the welt of emotion resting on Vanity's shoulders, deep within her heart.

"No, I think I just want some coffee," she could tell he was warming up to doing something for her birthday but she was not in the mood.

Winston, in a very soft, almost apologetic voice said, "I know it may not be a good time to celebrate, so I was going to just take you to get a bite and let you and Christina plan something later."

"We can do something on Sunday. Today I'm going over to Cole's to help her out." Vanity said as she sat staring at the mountaintops through the picture window.

"Would you like me to come?" Winston offered.

"No. I think I'll hang out in her room more and that would leave you with nothing to do." She replied.

"If you're sure, then I'll be here if you need me. I have some papers to grade. Happy Birthday." He came over and kissed her forehead. He laid a card on the counter next to the coffee pot.

"Thank you, Winston."

Winston left the kitchen and went into the library. When Winston had papers to grade that meant he would be in the library reading assignments all day, which left Vanity with an entire day to do her! She took her coffee up to her room and started pulling things out to put on. She planned to stop by the office to show her face and to give instructions for Michelle. Next on her list was to try to meet with Dexter for lunch to catch him up on what had been going on.

Before she headed to her shower, she powered up her cell phone and she had a text messages.

"Happy Birthday babe," it was Dexter.

"Thank you," she texted back. "Sorry about yesterday. Let's meet at your hotel for brunch and I'll tell you all about it."

"Sounds good. See you at 11." Dexter responded.

"Okay."

That left her a few hours to get things organized and to get down to the strip. After she picked out a cool outfit to wear, she showered. Afterward she called Cole to see what time would be good for a visit, but she did not answer so she called Robert and again, no answer. Vanity assumed they either were at the hospital or were just not up to calls. She logged a mental note to call her again later.

With not much evening prep, her hair was untamed so a sleek ponytail would have to do. As she started applying her mascara and looking into her eyes, she realized that, she was cheating on her husband. She stopped applying the mascara and stepped back from the mirror to look at her reflection. She had never considered cheating before and that did not mean there had not been opportunities, but she would never take anyone up on it, until now. What was so different about Dexter? Hell, he was a married man with kids – not the typical "good catch" at all. Granted he had made a name for himself, but that had never been a hook for her with anyone else. What was it?

She could not for the life of her see what he saw in her plump figure. As she looked at her full figure, she started to second-guess the outfit she picked out. It did not do anything for her. She put the compact down, went rummaging through her walk in closet looking for another outfit.

By the time she figured out what to wear, finished her makeup, and restyled her hair, she had wasted an hour and was now in a rush to get out of the house. She still had to stop by the office. Vanity checked in on Christina who was still asleep and left her a little note next to her cell phone. "Let's go to the movies later. I'll be home around three. Love mom."

She crept out and headed to the garage. "You look nice. You going over to Cole's dressed like that?" Winston asked.

"Oh no. I'm headed to the office for a bit. Cole didn't answer so I'll try her later." She had expected to leave unnoticed but that didn't happen.

"Well, if you want to have lunch, I'll swing by the office and pick you up." Winston stated, in a soft tone, almost wishing Vanity would say yes.

"That won't be necessary. We had an acquisition yesterday and I'll probably meet with the clients today over brunch. Thanks for the offer. I'll see you around 3." Vanity said as she attempted to leave.

"What's at 3?" Winston asked inquisitively.

"Chris and I will be going to the mall and movies. I have to come back to pick her up."

"Oh. Okay, well I'll see you then."

Vanity quickly went out the garage door before he asked her any more questions. When she drove down the street, she realized that Winston had looked at her in a way she had not seen before. It seemed to her to be a suspicious, unsure gaze. He knew she would never really meet with a new client wearing a casual outfit, but she did not want him surprising her at the office, so she had to tell him something. By the time she pulled into the office parking lot, her phone was ringing. It was Cole.

"Hello?"

"Hi Van." Cole said with the sound of tears in her voice.

"Cole, how are you?"

"Fine, we had to meet with the funeral home and get the arrangements started. I saw that you called." Cole replied.

"Yes, I wanted to come by and see if I could bring you anything."

"I guess I'm okay for now. I'm not up for any company. Thanks for offering." Cole said, sounding like sleep never came for her last night, and the tears she cried stained her heart.

"I will come by tomorrow, invited or not. I know you need some rest and I can help you get some things done around the house. Is Robert there?"

"Yes, he's right here." Cole replied.

"Let me speak to him."

"Hi, Vanity," Robert said.

"Robert, you know I know my sister. She has not slept since yesterday so you have to keep an eye on her. Get her in a hot bath with some lavender and give her a muscle relaxer. And make sure you call me if you need anything."

"I will," he responded in a dull tone.

"Okay, I'll see you guys tomorrow."

After they hung up the phone, she realized that he was just as out of it as she was. However, he had to be stronger for Cole and that meant making sure he kept her mind as clear as possible and she needed sleep. Vanity planned to see them no matter what the next day would bring.

When she got to the office, she called an emergency staff meeting to explain what was going on with Cole. The staff decided to put their money together and order food and a full house cleaning service for Cole and Rob. Vanity had Michelle work on those arrangements for the remainder of the day, and cancel all of her appointments. In her office, Vanity checked email and made sure that no other issues were brewing, but just as she started to get up to head out for brunch, she got a text.

"Are you on your way?"

She replied back, "No. I was just about to leave in a few minutes. Why?"

"My wife decided to show up and surprise me this weekend. She just arrived," he responded.

Vanity felt a lump in the bottom of her stomach, her lips parted, her mind blazed with thoughts. How crazy would that have been if she found them together? Vanity was not sure if his wife would remember her, but she did not need anything coming between this big deal. She texted back, "Dex, this is a sign we need to stop this."

"What? NO!" he responded.

"What do you mean NO? We cannot get caught and ruin everything." She hated to admit the truth but they were playing with fire and his wife's surprise visit was just the wakeup call she needed. Hell, Winston could have come down looking for her!

"Van, I cannot stop thinking about you. My mind is not on her. I am not happy about her being here and she knows it. I never invite her on a business trip. Call me, now. Please." Dexter almost sounded commanding, yet in real need of Vanity through his text.

Vanity pressed the call button almost without forethought of her surroundings, or even Dexter's proximity to his wife. She needed to get this talk hashed out. She had to put a stop to this.

"Van?"

"Yes, Dexter," her tone was short.

"I know you're upset about my attitude but it's nothing there between us. I want to be with you." Dexter said.

"I want to see you too but we both have families..."

"Hey, I know more than anyone what is at stake," he interrupted with irritation in his tone. "I'm not asking you to leave your husband, but I want to spend time with you. I need to spend time with you. I need to know you," he finished with sincerity.

Vanity felt her heart pumping, her blood racing to Dexter's words and the strength of his voice.

"Okay. If you can make a way today, let's see each other today, but this is the last time and I mean it."

"Fine. If that is how you feel, then at least I will be able to see you once more before we get *all* business from here on out." Dexter responded.

Vanity said, "Let's meet at Caesars this evening at nine."

"Can you meet earlier?" Dexter asked.

"I can't. My daughter and I are going to the mall and the theatre and I can't take a chance on being late."

"Okay, I'll see you at nine."

After they hung up, she sat back down at the desk. Staying at the office was not part of the plans; a quick call to Ms. Kim over at her spa was the first thing that she thought of. A nice manicure-pedicure was just what the doctor ordered. What a mess she had gotten herself into over the past few weeks. She had literally, fallen for a married man without any possibility of it actually materializing into something real. However, it felt so good to have someone desire her...want her. Dexter seemed to want her in a way she had only read about, fantasized for in her "personal" time, in bed alone. Winston had not taken any interest in her or made her feel desirable in years. She guessed that was the reason she halfway agreed to meet with Dexter tonight. She wanted to feel his touch and to have his energy connect with hers again. Even if they knew it would never be anything more, it was the thrill of having each other for any short period of time, which excited her.

****

During the movie, all she could think about was meeting up with Dexter in a couple hours. On the way home Vanity knew she did not want to go inside, "Chris, tell your father that I'll be in later. I have a few things to do." Christina nodded without looking up from her cell phone.

Vanity planned to stop by the office to freshen up for her date with Dexter. The office was Vanity's second home. She had all of the essentials to freshen up and look good for any second half of her day. Vanity had already changed clothes before the movies so her casual outfit was perfect for the impromptu date. She restyled her hair and reapplied her makeup. After getting ready, she called Caesars and made a reservation for a room. There was no chance that she wanted them to be seen together in a restaurant. After she made the reservation, she sent a text to Dexter to give him the room number.

"Are we still meeting?"

The time for his response seemed longer than usual, which only meant one thing, he was with her, and getting away could be a problem.

"Yes. What room are you in?" Dexter finally responded. The phone chirped again, before Vanity could respond back, "Meet me in the lobby. I will be there in 10 minutes." Dexter texted.

Vanity's response was ready, "Okay."

The moment Vanity pulled up at the hotel she had another bad feeling. Each time she felt bad about something, something bad was going to happen, did happen, or almost became a complete disaster. This time her senses were saying "WARNING DISASTER AHEAD."

Before going into Caesars', she sat in the car for a moment and just thought about what she had committed to doing. She was planning to go into this hotel and have sex with another man. The logical thing to do was to go, leave now before it went any further than it already had. That was the rational thing to do, the mature move to make.

However, the feeling Vanity felt while she was with him was out weighing the logical thing to do. Freeing the guilt and doubt from her mind, Vanity got out of the car and headed to the crowded lobby. Caesars' was one of the most popular original hotels on the strip; it was crowded all the time and gladly, today was no exception.

Vanity's phone vibrated as she walked into the lobby. It was a text from Winston. "Where are you?" He asked.

The first and only thought that came to Vanity after she read the text was, "Oh, shit!" The work excuse would have to do because there was truly no other acceptable explanation. This is the true sign of an amateur cheater that never had their shit together.

"I'm at the office," she responded back.

"When are you coming home? I wanted us to do something for your birthday." Winston asked.

"It's fine, I told you Sunday would be better." Vanity responded.

"Okay, don't be too late." Winston gave in.

As Vanity walked, she thought to herself, "Now, of all the times, he chose today to want to show me some attention."

Understandable, it was her birthday, but she was not concerned about it and Winston had not been in any previous years. Vanity wondered if he felt something was going on. That bad feeling came again, but she kept going.

She finally made it past the crowd to the concierge to be checked into her room. When she accepted the key from the concierge, and about to turn away, she felt a hand on the small of her back.

"What room can I escort you to ma'am?" She knew that voice. Even more, she knew that scent. It was Dexter.

"Oh, I don't know, sir. I'm not sure if I can allow a strange man to take me any place." Vanity replied over her shoulder with a semi seductive girlish grin.

"Well, let me introduce myself," he turned her around taking her hand like a queen, "I'm Dexter McKnight," he kissed the tip of her soft hand.

"Mr. McKnight, I am Vanity Christian Davis."

"It would be my pleasure to escort you safely to your penthouse." He said as he took the keycard and placed her hand inside his arm, "this way."

When they were inside the elevator, he pressed the "P" button. When the door of the elevator closed with no one else inside, he turned and kissed her so deeply that she could feel it in her panties. Instantly, she became aroused by his passionate kiss. When they arrived at the top floor his lips finished by teasing her neck as his fingertips rubbed her erect nipples. When they approached the room, they stopped and looked at each other. She spoke first.

"Dexter, what happens on the other side of this door is going to change us forever. There is no going back."

"I don't want to go back!" He teased.

Vanity said, "Are you serious? Once we cross this line, there is no turning back. I want this and I want you and I'm willing to risk a lot for this moment of passion with you."

"Damn, Vanity. It's like that?" He asked.

"Yes, it is," she spoke softly. "You make me feel something that no one has ever accomplished before, and the feeling, I can't lie, it makes me want to do things that I should never consider doing."

Dexter, looking into Vanity's eyes said, "Then, I'd be lying to you if I said I didn't feel the same way. I want this too and I have just as much to lose. Don't ever forget that. When we cross this line, we are doing it together."

She took the key and opened the door. The room was perfect. The view was fabulous. She took off her shoes and placed her handbag on the table in the foyer. She turned off her phone and went into the bedroom. Dexter placed his cell phone on the same table and joined her. Her body had not calmed down from the elevator kiss as she yearned for more. Dexter walked into the bedroom coming up behind her. He held her back to his already bare chest, kissing under Vanity's ear lobe with lips and tongue, moist and long. He knew this spot, she thought, "How did he know this spot?" Her mind began to close as her body opened. All she could do, all she wanted to do was embrace the feeling. He did not speak another word; little by little, he explored every part of her body. Slowly, he took his time to touch and listen to her moans, gasps and sights. Gradually, Dexter peeled away the layers of clothing that she came in with until Vanity stood before him, naked, wet, horny, and hungry for him. Vanity wanted to feel his lips on her nipples, sucking, pulling them, and licking each one until they were engorged. His lips and tongue left no suspense to his intent. Dexter wanted to make her wetter than she had ever been, wetter than her own fingers could or would ever feel her get. He was doing exactly that. Dexter purposely kept his fingers from the prize; all he wanted to use was his tongue. He licked every inch of her as she stood before him, tasted every part of her while Vanity's legs trembled. He did all of this and yet never touched her already soaking pussy. Dexter had a plan and he was working it to perfection. He backed off and in a commanding, sexy voice said, "Lay down on your stomach." Vanity felt hazy from the pleasure her body was receiving. Dexter's soft, gentle, erotic tongue bath almost made her cum. She heard his voice and listened to his commanding tone, without thought to his purpose she laid down and Dexter wasted no time in following her into the sheets. His tongue and lips moved with skill and ease down the back of Van's neck, slowly down her spine as his fingers massaged her sides. He wasn't missing an inch of Van. He wanted her to know lust and pleasure from all angles. He wanted her to have a buildup of anticipation that would explode in orgasmic pleasure. It was coming, his sexual plan was forming, and he could hear it in Van's ohhhs and ahhhs. Dexter smiled to himself because he wanted to give her pleasure, as she had never known before. He wanted to be the man that sexually released her secret passion. It was working. He tasted every part of her from behind. Dexter touched and tasted areas that Van had thought, "That's not it" became, "Oh damn, ohhh," when her back arched and his tongue spread her ass. In one swift motion, almost on cue, as Dexter backed off, Van turned over and she placed her hand between her thighs and felt her wetness. "Shit, my pussy never felt this wet," she thought. Her fingers did not stop rubbing softly over her clit, as Dexter watched Vanity explore her throbbing clit. Dexter said, "You like to play with her I see."

Which was more of a statement from Dex than a question, yet Vanity did not feel embarrassed by his gaze, actually turned on even more. She simply said, "Yes."

He kissed her thighs and spread her legs to make his way to her running water. His lips were so warm that with each kiss it sent a shock wave through her body. His tongue licked the bottom half of her pussy lips first, then came his lips to suck her in, Van never felt this strange sensation before, not from this part of her pussy, but Dexter knew things, he was a true cunnilingus. He slide upward spreading her lips open, releasing some of the juice that was trying to escape from the overflow, the juice Dexter's lips had been sucking in with skill, as his tongue found nerve endings Vanity never knew existed. Vanity's voice heavy and hard said, "You're so nasty." As his tongue softly flicked the hood of Van's clit, to expose its fullness, his perfectly manicured finger entered her, and found its way to one spot, one throbbing area up under her clitoris. It was time. He felt it. He moved his tongue in rhythm with his finger, "Oh shit!" screamed Vanity, "ahhhh, shit!" She let out again. Dexter's fingers glazed coated with Van's juice. She was coming just the way he wanted her to. Van grabbed the top of Dexter's head, the sides of his face; she threw her hands back and began grinding her fat, wet swollen pussy on his lips as his tongue stayed firmly on her clit. Moving faster, swifter, rotating her clit into erotic sensations. He made her pelvis spread; her pussy muscle throbbed without control. Van screamed, "Yes...fuck me with your tongue!" She screamed into the pillow she grabbed from beneath her head.

Dexter enjoyed the response from Vanity to his tongue work, he enjoyed hearing her erotic chants to the point of his dick becoming as hard as its nine-inch length would allow.

Vanity's orgasm was thick and strong, leaving her legs in a consistent tremble, her heart pounding as she felt the blood in her body flowing like a river run wild. Dexter wanted to feel this pleasure on the head of his dick, flowing down the shaft. He was ready to enter her warmest place with strength, but slowly, so he could feel the fatness within her pussy. As his face emerged from between Vanity's thighs, she could see her joy, her wetness covering his lips, his chin and he smiled as if a child coming in from the hottest day of the year to cold water. His smile made her think that he looked like he wanted to say "Thank you for that refreshing drink", but not a word uttered from him. Dexter climbed Vanity to a full mount, as he spread her legs wide, his thick ready dick went in slowly, just as he was planning, just as he wanted her, slowly. His stroke started with ease, like a soft playing rhythm, like his tongue and finger. Vanity felt his firmness deep in her; she felt his strength keeping her legs spread as his dick worked her dripping wet pussy. She was building up to cum again.

"Oh damn, that feels good, damn my pussy...oooohhhhh, fuck..." tears streamed down Vanity's face, but pleasure was on her mind, pleasure rest within her pussy, and she loved Dexter's pleasure tools. As he stroked harder, he quickly pulled her legs together and placed them both over one shoulder, almost turned sideways and his dick did not miss a beat, his heart pumped with a fierceness that rivaled any cardio workout. Dexter wanted to come in her. He wanted Vanity to be filled with him, to blend with her. Yes, that's what he was going to do, nut inside of her.

Harder he stroked, trying to get so deep in her that the head of his throbbing dick could feel her uterus. "Fuck me Vanity, fuck me. Give me this pussy, tell me you want my dick." Vanity was no slouch to fucking, as a younger woman she had had her fair share of erotic nights. She blew the dust off and showed him what her pussy could truly do.

Vanity pulled her legs from Dexter's shoulders grabbed him and said, "Lay your ass down," Dexter's eyes opened wide but he followed instructions, laid back and Vanity, holding the base of Dexter's dick, sucked it one long stroke with tongue and lips at the same time, till the head popped like a cork from a champagne bottle. POP! The sound escaped from her lips. Holding his dick, with a firm grip, straight and stiff, she mounted him in one full sweep.

Vanity rode this dark skinned man like a bull, making his leg muscles flutter, his toes crack and his voice sounding like, well like this, "ahhh, ohhh, yyyyesssss..." She gave him what he wanted. Pinching and pulling on his nipples, rubbing on his thick chest, riding his firm cock, she gave him the fuck he needed, the fucking that he thought he could give to her...she gave to him.

Dexter's cum was strong, and she could feel her pussy muscle squeezing down to extract every ounce, she could feel him coming in her and she wanted it. Vanity wanted to drain his pipe while she watched his face grimace, contort and finally smile like that child who smiled from getting that special treat. He did! She was so pleased with her efforts, to herself, she said, "You go girl!"

As Vanity lay fully forward on Dexter's chest, her fingers played with the hairs, and not a sound came from them for what seemed like an eternity. Vanity replayed the highlights of this intense session, remembering how their squeaks and moans matched. What a beautiful sound.

The silence was broken "Damn Van, I could have never predicted that," he said.

Vanity did not say a word. She smiled but he could not see it.

"Vanity, you are amazing."

"Well, I don't know about all of that. I intended to have more fun but I've been so tense."

"Hey, no worries, we have time for more."

"Is that so? Don't you have to get back to...?"

He interrupted her by putting his finger over her lips. "Let's not talk about the future, let's just stay in this moment for a while."

Vanity said nothing more. Her mind was still fighting between present and future. How does life go back to normal after this? Dexter was not someone who she could forget and go back to her life as usual. "His wife, my husband, our children, they would be devastated if they found out," she thought.

She tried to push those thoughts aside and as soon as she felt she was successful, Dexter's phone rang from the foyer.

"I think you better get that," Vanity said as she tried to dismount from Dexter's body but he stopped her.

"Vanity, how many times do I have to tell you? I'm in this moment with you. Nothing else matters to me right now. I am enjoying you too much to be interrupted." He said.

"It could be an emergency," Vanity said, with somewhat of a surprised look on her face.

"Baby, we're in Vegas. For all they know I am drunk at a casino bar right now." The phone only rang that one time. Within minutes, their breathing became in unison. She rested her thoughts and fell asleep.

****

The next sound she heard was a knock at the door, "room service."

"Oh, shit!" Vanity jumped up, looked at the clock, and realized it was morning. Dexter was nowhere in sight. "Dexter!" she called out.

"Hey, babe," he came rushing in to see what was wrong. "Are you okay?" He asked

"What's going on? We were supposed to check out last night! This is bad! My husband is never going to believe this lie."

Vanity gathered her things and ran off to the bathroom to shower. She slammed the door behind her. This was definitely the beginning of the end. She could feel it.

Dexter came to the door, "Van, I'm sorry but I overslept, too. I just wanted to close my eyes for a minute." He said.

"It's not your fault. Please, just go ahead and leave. I'll talk to you later."

"Are you sure? I ordered some breakfast if you want it." He asked.

"Thanks."

Within a few minutes, she heard the door close. Vanity took a quick shower and was in and out of the room within twenty minutes. She could not even think about eating anything. As she left the hotel, something in her said she should go to the office. No one should be there. Vanity thought that the office was her best move, yes, everyone knew her passion for work, knew how relaxed making deals and decisions made her. That was the plan, go to the office and work. When she turned the corner, there was a police car in the parking lot.

"What the hell?" she thought.

Behind the cruisers, she saw Winston's car. "Oh, shit!" He must have called the police when she did not come home last night. She pulled into the parking lot and saw Winston's face light up.

He ran over to her car, "Where have you been? I've been calling you all night and your phone is going straight to voicemail," he demanded an answer.

She was getting out of the car, "Why are these police here?" She sounded casual.

"You were missing, Vanity! Where have you been?" Winston asked again.

"Missing? I wasn't missing. Some friends were in town and we partied a little too much. I crashed at Caesars," she said nonchalantly.

"You could have called to tell me that Vanity. We were worried sick! This is unacceptable behavior.

You're too damn old to be running up and down the strip like some damn teenager!" Winston yelled in a tone and manner Vanity had not heard in years.

The police officer came over to try to calm Winston down. He was getting a little irate, agitated, and Vanity thought the officer looked at him as an angry and hostile black man. Instead of defending herself, she stood there like a chastised kid, to avoid getting him arrested.

The officer said, "Sir, I'm going to need you to calm down. Your wife seems to be fine. Be thankful that nothing bad happened."

"Happy? I'm not happy. I'm pissed!" Vanity jumped in attempting to deflect the officer from Winston and putting a lid on this situation before the pot boiled over.

"Winston, please calm down. I am sorry for being out all night but it was my birthday and I got a call and..."

"Your birthday huh? It seems like you would rather run the streets than to spend time with your husband on your birthday." Dexter said.

"Look!" she could not hold it any longer, "I am not going to stand here any further and allow you to chastise me like a child. I said I was sorry. I am going home."

She immediately got back in her car and sped off. The officer and Winston stood in the parking lot as she drove away. From the rearview mirror, it looked like they shook hands and parted ways.

Vanity pulled out her phone and realized it was still off. She powered it up and gave Christina a call. That was the last person she wanted worried about her.

"Hey mom! Are you okay?" Christina asked.

"Yes, baby. I'm sorry I worried you. I was with some friends and lost track of time."

"Are you on your way home?"

"In a bit. I have to make a stop first."

"Dad has been worried. He called the police."

"Yea, I know. I've spoken to your father."

"Is everything alright between you two?" Christina asked.

"What makes you say that, sweetie?"

Christina, in an even toned voice responded, "It just seems like you two are distant."

"Well Chris, you're right. We have become distant but I don't want to worry you about that. You focus on college and your future. Your dad and I will be fine."

"I just want you both to be happy, mom." Christina said.

"Thank you baby. That means a lot. Tell your dad I'll be home in a while."

"Okay."

Vanity had no errand to run. She was just avoiding going home and being in the same room, same space, and same house with Winston. After last night, any ounce of emotion she had left in her for Winston was gone. There was nothing there. They were roommates with a license. She could not take it any longer. Vanity pulled into the mall parking lot and gave Cole a call.

"Hey Van," Cole answered.

"Hi sis. How are you?"

"I'm okay. I got a call from Winston looking for you. What was that about?" Cole asked.

"Oh, girl a lot about nothing. We just had a little miscommunication."

"Oh." Cole responded.

"Yeah, no need to worry." Vanity tried to say in a reassuring voice.

"We've made funeral arrangements for next Tuesday," Cole, offered the information before Vanity had to ask.

"Okay. Do you need my help with anything?"

"No. Our parents came in this morning to help out so we're fine." Cole said.

"I wanted to stop by tomorrow for a bit. Are you up to it?"

"Actually, I am. Can you run me to a few stores?"

Cole asked.

"Sure. I'll be over around noon."

"Okay. Thanks sis." Cole said.

"You bet."

After she hung up from Cole, a text from Dexter came through.

"Hope you're not mad at me."

"Of course not. You did nothing wrong," she texted back.

"My flight leaves for Denver in 4 hours, I would like to see you before I leave," he responded.

Vanity had no further intention of holding a text conversation with Dexter. Inside her, she wanted to hear his voice. She called him.

"I don't think that's a good idea." Van said.

"Why not?" asked Dexter

"Where could we meet?" she asked.

"At your office. No one is there right?" Dexter suggested.

"No, it should be empty today." She answered.

"Meet me there in one hour." Dexter said.

Vanity smiled at his happy tone about their agreement to meet. She thought that she was insane because literally hours ago, Winston was in her face, yelling about where had she been and here she is again putting herself in situations that could only get worse.

Love, Fire & Ice

Before leaving the mall, Vanity wasted a little time browsing through several stores, but her mind, was somewhere else. She was going through so many emotions mentally, sadness for the loss of her goddaughter, love and lust from a man that she knew she should maintain a business and professional relationship with, and anger toward Winston.

In one of her favorite boutiques, she found a cute outfit to change into at the office. She felt like she was on cloud nine for a moment, and even when the moment was sometimes fleeting, when her thoughts were on Dexter, cloud nine was her residence.

Vanity loved the way he made her feel because she had the freedom to be her. Unfortunately, Dexter was not hers and probably never would be, so just as quickly as she was on cloud nine, reality returned and she knew that this meeting had to be the end. This had to stop. After the incident with Winston and Dexter's wife popping up she had to put an end to it before one of them found out and everyone involved got hurt.

Three

The hour came around quickly. Before Vanity knew it, she was pulling into the parking lot, and Dexter's rental car was already there. She did not have time to change into her outfit. She felt bad that she still had the same clothing on from last night. However, that became an afterthought the moment she got out of her car and headed toward the building. A public greeting was not in order so she went straight to the door. Once the doors were unlocked, she motioned for Dexter to come in, she wanted to be extra careful, and lock the door behind them. As soon as they entered her office door, he picked her up and sat her on the oversized executive desk in her office. Dexter wanted to undress her, take her on the desk, he wanted to taste her on his tongue and lips, as Vanity dripped her juice to his pussy eating skills, he wanted to feel the wetness of her pussy on his dick, he wanted both of them to orgasm together.

"Wait, Dexter! What are you doing?" Vanity said breathing heavily.

"What does it look like I'm doing?" He asked.

"I know what you're doing, but we cannot do this here," she said as she pushed his hands away.

"Come on Van, let me taste you, feel you again." He begged.

"Wait. What about what I want?"

"Hey, I'm sorry. I thought you were down with this," he stopped and stood up.

"Dexter, I wanted to talk to you because last night and today was a close call. My husband was here waiting at my office when I stopped by this morning. He had the police thinking I was missing since I didn't answer any of his phone calls last night."

"Missing?" said Dexter in a puzzled voice.

"Yes, I turned off my phone. I wasn't supposed to spend the night, remember!"

"Oh, right...I can see why he thought that." Dexter said.

"Exactly, so we can't keep doing this. What about your wife, did she ask you anything about your whereabouts? Where did she think you were all night?" Vanity asked, but she did not really want the answer to her question.

"I told you, they thought I was at a casino." Dexter replied in a low tone, as he looked away.

"Well that doesn't change anything," said Vanity, "We can't keep this up. It's too risky."

"Oh, it's risky? You think loving you, wanting to be with you is just risky? Vanity, I..." Dexter's usually assured and controlled voice broke, "I can't stop loving you, I could never return to life as it was, not like this, not just like that." Dexter showed real emotion, his word touched a chord in Vanity.

Vanity slowly walked over to Dexter, his back to her hiding the whelp of emotion that was very visible on his face and in his voice.

Softly she said, "We are married...to other people. Our lives and the lives of others must matter, it has to be a factor in how we proceed, or end. Don't you get it?"

"I do get it and *we* should be married, to each other." Dexter said.

There was no rebuttal from Vanity, Dexter took her in his arms and with passion and lust, and kissed her deeply. Vanity felt the heat from his embrace the passion from his lips on hers. In his arms Vanity felt herself slip away, intoxicated by the moment, moistened by the love she felt pouring through Dexter's lips. Wanting to push Dexter away was the right thing to do, but she couldn't. Vanity knew the rest of their lives could not be this way, she knew that if this was going to be real they had to have more than this, and more than a moment but she couldn't stop. She couldn't walk away.

"Dexter, I hope we know what we're doing. I want to trust you, but I'm scared."

"Van, I'm not living in the moment, you are my moments, and you are my future. Shit is messed up with our marriages, I know, but we can change that, together we can find happiness and peace in each other. I am not thinking about my wife and I'm sure as hell not thinking about your husband. It's just us right now."

"That all sounds good Dexter but we know what the reality is."

"Do we?" he asked.

"We're playing with our lives, Dex."

"I know..."

That was the last thing he said before he picked her up and carried her to the leather sofa. It had been slept on several nights before but this had never happened. She could not get over how well maintained he was. Nothing funny about him, he was real, solid and she could feel it. His touch sent electricity through her body. How did he do that? All Vanity was sure of at this moment was how good it felt to be touched in a way that she wanted to be touched and with no inhibitions she could let go and be who she wanted to be.

"Vanity?"

"Hmm?" she said with her eyes still closed.

"What is the one thing that you want me to do for you?" He asked.

"Huh?" she said aloud, and then she thought, "Did he just ask me what I wanted?" Over the past umpteen years, she had not had the pleasure of getting her way in the bedroom. It had been such a routine that she could do everything with her eyes closed and her mind on a million and one other things.

"Well, I don't know. Why don't you just surprise me."

Vanity had been so out of the sex scene that she did not know what to ask for. One thing she did know is that there was nothing he did to her body, it didn't respond to and she suspected that it would not start now.

His hands slowly found their way to her bra strap. As he unhooked it, he cupped her breast and immediately gave them attention. His lips, his tongue, sucked and licked liked he practiced on a charms lollipop. Vanity's nipples became rock hard and with every stroke of his tongue, she felt a tingle on her pussy.

"Hmm, damn, that's so good; you make me feel so damn good."

She was wet and getting hornier by the second. Dexter knew it, but he did not move from her nipples, not yet. He paid particular attention to the right nipple sucking it as his tongue drew designs on the top of it.

Vanity's pussy throbbed, she felt pleasure cramps through her pelvis, electrical fire tingled and burned in her. She wanted his lips on her clit, she wanted him to suck and gently nibble at the hood, but her voice could not come out to tell him. Dexter repositioned himself and at the same time put Vanity into a complete lay down position. He spread Vanity's thighs with strength and hunger, as if to feed from her, with force, he thrust his face forward. This sudden motion gave Vanity a lump in her throat, her heart pounded as his tongue found her clit, swollen, ready to be taken. Dexter's tongue was like a vibrator, skillfully buzzing with the right amount of pressure that kept Vanity's clit sensitive to lick, suck and pull. He seemed to hold the hood back as far as it could go with his upper lip while his tongue brought out her clit to full engorgement. Vanity's entire pussy was on fire. A heat burned from deep in her coming straight through her love lips and onto Dexter's. The heat made his dick throb...made his mind search for ways to please her pussy. He heard the soft moans from Vanity, felt her nails digging into his skin, her hands unsure of whether to grab his shoulder, his head or the pillow. In Dexter's mind he was speaking to himself, "Yes, Vanity that's it, give me that multiple orgasm that my lips want, baby! Cum, for me..."

On cue, Vanity did oblige his lustful desires. She came hard, her pussy muscles convulsing, spasms racing through her uterus and into her stomach. Her juice was like cream, thick, fresh cream that Dexter licked up before it ran down her ass. This time he did not enter her with his tongue, oh no, he wanted the juice that lay in her for his dick's pleasure. As Vanity let out her last deep moan, almost a scream, Dexter swiftly pulled his body forward to place the head of his thick dick on her clit; his shaft spread her lips and ass. He stroked her this way, again she moaned, this time sounding like a bird, as she grinded her swollen pussy on his thick cock. Dexter had rhythm; he was truly skilled in the art of grinding, so much so that Vanity felt a soft gentle orgasm building from this erotic act. She remembered college, always being horny, girl secrets, girls night out, too many drinks, touching exploring, grinding. The memories and his movement made her wetter, made her come again and again as her thighs wrapped around his back to press him deeper between her pussy lips, to feel the head of his cock electrify her clit.

She said softly in his ear, "Fuck me now, give me that dick, and make this pussy spread open for you."

He smiled, as his shaft did her bidding. His deep slow stroke sent a shiver through Vanity that she had never felt before from any cock or toy for that matter. She felt herself coming again on his dick; he felt the juice covering his cock. This made Dexter pump harder, faster, as her vaginal walls exploded in waves of juice that ran down his balls. He loved that feeling; he loved feeling the insides of this pussy. Dexter stroked and stroked to Vanity's rhythm, as he pulled her into a seated position on him. His knees under her, his hand clutching her ass, his strength lifted her up and down on his dick, he was fully in her, and she loved taking him in, Vanity pushed Dexter backward to mount him. Her ass went up and down hard on his dick, she saw joy and lust as his face contorted, heard his toes crack as he gasped in a pelvic spasm, he was coming for her. She could feel the thick vein pressed on the lower portion of her pussy throbbing, she knew she should pull off, she thought of taking him in her mouth as he nut, but she wanted to feel his cum in her, wanted him to release his seed so they could blend together. Dexter obliged. He came in her as if tomorrow were not promised; as if this were the last time that sex would be had between man and woman.

She thought, "He came in me, damn, he came in me." She kissed his lips, tasted herself on him, and smiled.

They sat in a comfortable silence until Vanity's cell phone interrupted them. The moment was gone.

****

By the time she arrived home, it was close to dusk. The sun was setting and the sky was a burnt orange, there was peace in the air as she came down her street, but when she pulled into the driveway, the calmness she felt in the atmosphere quickly dissipated as reality settled in, and the fantasy she had with Dexter was gone. The life she lived with her husband was her reality. Why had she settled for such a life? Did she see something that was not there? She knew she was not happy even though the lifestyle that she lived would not give anyone that indication. She wanted for nothing. So she thought. What was missing? It would be easy to say that Dexter was the answer. He was new and fresh in her life. What would happen when this thing they had gotten old, familiar? Would she be unhappy all over again? So many questions went through her head as she made her way from the car to the house. Still in her thoughts as she entered from the garage, Vanity was startled by Winston sitting at the table in the dark. She turned on the light.

"What's going on Van?" Winston asked.

Vanity could not tell if he was angry or hurt but he asked as if he already knew the answer would not be anything he wanted to hear.

"Oh, I had some things to take care of at..."

"No," he said interrupting her, "I mean with you. Why are you staying out like this?"

She approached the table but did not pull out a chair. She stood there with a blank look on her face, "I'm going through some things right now, and I just need to sort them out."

"What things?" he questioned.

"I'm tired and don't want to talk about it."

"What? Why not? You've obviously been out enjoying yourself. You're not answering your phone; you're changing outfits while you're out." He had questions, too many for Vanity to logically answer or explain.

"Damn. He had started noticing things," she thought. "As soon as he sees me doing the things I want to do, because I am not doing anything with him, he has something to say. Next he'll say I'm wearing my hair different."

Almost on cue, Winston said, "And your hair and makeup are different."

This was crazy. Feeling guilty, yet holding her confidence, she refused to stand there listening to Winston questions and quasi accusations.

"I told you that I don't want to talk about it."

Salty, Winston said in a low slow voice, "Is it another man?"

Vanity did not know why surprise filled her, or if it was the tone in his voice. Without a response, without a word said in confirmation or denial, she walked out of the kitchen, and went up to the loft. She was nervous, fidgeting with her fingers, staring blankly at her phone, her mind raced because she knew he already had his suspicions. Vanity did not want to face the truth of her own mess, not yet. Besides, she was not going to give Winston the pleasure of figuring this all out so fast. She felt confusion turn to anger; she thought, "Who was he to start questioning me all of a sudden?" Just the thought of that made her neck sweat!

She stripped from her clothes, tucked her panties mid-laundry basket, and headed for a cool shower. As she released her hair from its ponytail and let the cool water run through it, she thought of Dexter, not of their last encounter, but how she felt about this new man in her life, what he had opened in her closed world. She thought about how it would end and what she would return to when he was gone. She began crying, she felt like a woman that had known and lost the love of her life, she stood in the shower and wept. Questioning her crying, her weeping, she came to the conclusion that the weeping came from the thought that she had given herself to another man who was not her husband and she could never get that back. The purity of her marriage, no matter how stale it was; was gone. The anger came from the fact that she had allowed most of her adult life to pass by and half of it had been spent unhappily married. It was amazing how the world turned. Was Vanity making up for lost time? Regardless of the truth, Dexter made her feel like she was.

Winston came into the bathroom interrupting her moment and she quickly wiped her face. There was nothing to talk about and if he saw her crying, he would continue to pry. She had to get him out of there.

"What is it now, Winston?" she snapped.

"What is bothering you Vanity?"

"I told you that I don't want to talk about it. I have a lot on my plate. We can talk tomorrow."

"Tomorrow?" He asked.

"Yes! Tomorrow!"

All she heard was the door slam. A silent sigh of relief escaped her. Facing the truth was not part of the plan tonight because she knew it meant that Winston would be hurt and the tailspin would begin. No matter how much she felt the marriage had become stagnant; that did not give her the right to let things go down this way. An overwhelming feeling of guilt filled her. She had to figure out how to fix this. How she planned to accomplish that was a different story.

The next morning she had hoped that Winston would be gone but he was not. He was actually in the kitchen reading the paper, was he just waiting for her to come in, or was he really reading the paper? She was unsure which. There was no plan figured out yet so whatever she told him would still be a lie. Moreover, at this point, the truth was something she was still struggling with and telling Winston anything of the sort would just make things worse.

"Good morning," she managed to say grabbing her favorite mug down from the cabinet and poured a cup of decaf.

"Good morning," he said.

After she added creamer and sugar, she went into the den to check her email. She felt like she had gained a few more minutes since he did not say anything while she prepared her coffee. Before Vanity logged on to the computer, she called Cole to make sure she was still up to company.

"Good morning, Van."

"Hey sis. You still up to going to a few stores today?"

"Well, actually I have to go to the hospital. They performed an autopsy and the results are not back yet. We may be pushing back the funeral."

"Why?"

"Yeah, they won't release the death certificate until the results come back this week," Cole said.

"Okay. Well, if you want to get out just let me know. I want to get you caught up on things at the office, if you're up to it."

"Actually, that would be good. I need to start moving around. I feel myself slipping and I know getting back to work will help me. My doctor is already suggesting medication for postpartum and you know how I feel about that crap." Cole spoke in a matter of fact voice.

"Yea, and if I have anything to do with it; you will not get on those medications. They make things worse before they get better."

"I know. So maybe I will come into the office Tuesday just to get out of the house. Please let the office know to just let me get through it...you know?" Cole asked.

"Yes, I know what you mean. I'll have your favorite cup of latte when you get in. I miss you girl!"

"Aww, I miss you too, sis. See you in the morning." Cole said as they hung up from each other.

After they hung up, she realized that Winston had been standing in the doorway of the den.

"Were you listening to my conversation?" She said with an attitude.

"No, I wasn't." Winston exclaimed.

"Then why are you just standing there?"

"I was waiting on you to get off the phone so that I could ask you a question," Winston said.

"What? What is it Winston?"

"Well since you're not in the mood to talk to me like you were so happy to talk to Nicole, then I will come back to you later." Winston turned and walked away.

"Fine. I have some things to do today."

"Christina is flying out in the morning and she was hoping that we could all go have dinner tonight." Winston said this with his back to Vanity, as he strolled up the back staircase.

"That's fine. I will return around five o'clock."

He stopped. "Where are you going?"

"I have some errands to run."

"What kind of errands?" He asked.

"Look Winston, do not start questioning my every move. If you have something to say, just say it. I don't have time for these fifty questions."

Love, Fire & Ice

Winston could see the agitation, the anger in Vanity. He came back down stairs and said, "Vanity, I am sure there is something going on with you. These last couple of weeks, you've been away from the office, staying out late and spending less time at home."

"Well at least you didn't say, spending less time with you because you spend so much time at the school that we never spend time together anyway. But now all of a sudden you start noticing that I've started doing more things by myself."

"Is that what this is about? My being away too much so now you're going to start running the streets of Vegas like a twenty-one year old." He proclaimed.

"Excuse me?" She said aloud then thought, "How dare he belittle my needs, my time spent, or what I need to do for myself as a woman."

Dexter said, "I am not going to argue with you Vanity. I want to know what's going on with you and you are finding every reason to avoid the conversation. Either you're going to tell me what's going on or I'll badger it out of you."

"Oh, okay," she responded in an unconvincing tone.

"Yes. I know I am always at the school and not here, but I do my best to make time when you ask for it." He stated.

"When I ask for it, huh?"

"Yes, but you don't see me in the streets all hours of the night." Winston said.

"Winston, please. You're at the school more than you are at home. I don't know what you're doing."

Startled by Vanity's boiled assertion, Winton said, "What are you saying? You think I am cheating on you. Is that what this is about?" He asked with a measure of anger in his voice.

"I am not saying that. But you obviously find more things and reasons to be at that school than you do here at home. So, I started to realize that maybe I should be finding more things to do."

"What are you saying Vanity? Just be plain and clear with me, can you do that? You have always spent just as much time at VanCole as I have at the college." He said.

"What do you mean, what am I saying? I'm saying don't start looking down my throat just because I am starting to find things that I want to do without you."

With that stark statement, Winston walked into the den and sat on the sofa. He looked out the bay window that faced their favorite mountain and sat in silence for a few moments. Vanity did not say anything more because she knew what was next. He would stay quiet for a while then wait for her to walk out of the room or he would. The conversation would be over and they would go back to their normal lives. Nothing resolved.

On the surface she had escaped the current situation, and only because she was able to turn the tables on him. Yes, it was wrong but he was a contributor to what she was feeling about their marriage and she refused to let him think he was a saint. It was not his fault that she cheated. She made that choice on her own but dammit, she needed a certain type of attention and he was just not giving it to her. Winston's cell phone rang out from the kitchen and off he went. From the sound of the conversation, it was a student. Moments later, he was gone, on his way to the school, as usual.

He did not say a word on his way out but she really didn't expect him to, he never really did anyway. He would come and go as he pleased. He was usually gone early every morning, even on some weekends to the school helping a student with some project or paper and she would be home or at the office doing her own thing. It was how they lived, which is funny how now that her life had started to take a turn he wanted to start being her husband and attentive.

"Damn you Winston, it's too late!" she spoke aloud.

The birthday dinner with Winston and Christina made her reflect on her life. She enjoyed motherhood; she raised Christina to be a responsible and wise young adult. When it was time for college, she was ready and had her plan. If there was anything she did not regret about her life with Winston, it was being a mother to their daughter and above all, she felt that Christina was the one thing they did right, together.

The next morning after an eventful evening, Vanity got dressed for the office. Nothing big on her calendar except to check with her staff on the campaign for the McKnight firm. They were expected back in Vegas in a few weeks to discuss the plans to break ground for the new restaurant.

When she got to the office Michelle was already busy, "Hi Mrs. Davis, you had a package delivered this morning. It's on your desk."

"Thanks and how are you this morning?"

"I am outstanding." Michelle was a bright and chipper young woman. A great project coordinator and the best at what she did. Michelle, a college student majoring in project management, was exactly what they needed running such a busy operation. She kept Vanity and Nicole on their toes.

"By the way, Mr. McKnight from McKnight Enterprises called and requested a conference call with you this morning. Your calendar was free so I scheduled it for 10 am."

"Thanks, Michelle."

Vanity made a mental note to do something nice for Michelle. She had really picked up the slack with Cole being out and covering for her pop up meetings with Dexter.

In Vanity's office, Michelle had already pulled back the Venetian blinds; they both admired the sunshine as it peered through. The package Michelle mentioned was on the corner of her desk. It was from Tiffany's the jewelry store. After a quick mental retail check, she realized that she had not ordered from Tiffany's in months. Vanity sat down at her desk looking at the package, trying to figure out who sent it. In mid thought, her phone rang.

"VanCole, this is Vanity speaking."

"Yes, Vanity my name is Francine McKnight and my husband ordered a product from Tiffany's and had it delivered to a Vanity Davis. Is that you?"

"Your husband?"

"Yes, my husband, Dexter McKnight. Do you know him?" Francine McKnight asked.

Vanity's heart sank.

"Oh my god! This was Dexter's wife. What in the hell had he done now!" She thought.

This package was from Dexter. "How stupid of him," she thought. He had to know that his wife could easily check the credit card statements.

"Yes, I know Mr. McKnight, he's a new client."

"Did you get a package from Tiffany's?" Francine asked.

"Actually, my assistant did state a package arrived, but I had not had an opportunity to open it. Is there a problem?"

"Problem? Well, yes there is a problem. My husband sent a $2,500 gift to a new business associate. I have a problem with that. Something isn't right and I'm going to find out what it is!" She hung up the phone.

Well that did not take long. His wife was already on his tail. Men were so weak at cheating it was, pathetic. Hell, Vanity wasn't any better, but she would never do anything as obvious as this. Why would he send a gift like that? Vanity did not want to know what the gift was. His wife was upset and it made her upset. She called Dexter.

"Hi Vanity!" He said with a smile in his voice. He was probably feeling good about his gift antic.

"Dexter, what on earth were you thinking?"

"What? You don't like them?" Dexter asked.

"I haven't even opened the package."

"What? Why not?"

"Because Francine just called asking me questions about a package delivered here from Tiffany's!"

"What the hell! How did she know that?" Dexter questioned himself aloud.

"Apparently, she is going through your credit card statements and figured it out once the delivery was confirmed."

"What did you say?" Dexter asked.

"I told her that we are new business associates and I played off the package as if it wasn't anything special."

"She must have been tracking the package and wondering why it wasn't coming to her. Dammit. This is going to be an interesting conversation." Dexter said.

"I'm sure. I'm surprised she hasn't called you yet."

"Well open the package, Vanity." Dexter told her.

She grabbed the box and cut her way through the exterior package with her monogram letter opener to see the signature teal blue box with the white bow on it. The most exquisite yellow diamond studs she had ever seen glistened before her.

"Well?" he said.

"They are stunning."

"I hope that means you like them." His voice held a smile of accomplishment.

"I love them...but Dexter, we're getting messy and your wife will find out that this is not a business gift. She knows something is up and she's going to figure it out."

"Vanity, I want to see you in those studs when I return to Vegas in a few weeks." Dexter said.

"You're serious about continuing to see me aren't you?"

"You damned right I am." Dexter proclaimed with confidence.

After that she heard his intercom over the phone state that his wife was there waiting to see him. She knew that conversation would get ugly just like hers was this morning.

"Sounds like you're about to get your ear full."

"I think so." He said without a layer of fear in his voice.

"Talk to you later." Vanity said.

"Definitely. This should be an interesting day."

She sat with the box in her hand staring at the earrings. She had dozens of studs but these were unlike any she had ever bought for herself let alone received as a gift. On the other hand, maybe it was because they were from Dexter that she adored them so much. All she knew was they were going to be noticeable if she wore them. They were flawless. Wait a minute. She could not wear these $2,500 earrings from Dexter. She must have lost her mind. The more she got into this thing with Dexter, the more things got messy. How was he going to explain this purchase to his wife? Better yet, how was his wife going to feel about the business relationship after this? All of these questions were nothing compared to what Winston would think if he saw her in the diamond studs. Normally he would not notice but he was on high alert, watching out for every little change that Vanity came home with.

The conference call planned with the McKnight firm did happen. His associates and Vanity's team discussed the campaign progress and some other details as expected. After the meeting was over, Dexter sent Vanity a text message that said, "Call me."

She did, immediately, "Hello."

"Hi, Van. We need to talk," he said.

"About what?"

"The earrings. I need you to send them back to me," He stated.

"Why?"

"Because I had to tell my wife that those were meant for her, but somehow my secretary sent them to the wrong address."

"Oh, really? You're an Indian Giver, huh?" she teased.

"Come on, Van. You know I don't want to ruffle any feathers with her right now. Business is going too well and I don't need her messing anything up. I'll make it up to you, I promise." He attempted to reassure her.

"No need. I'm just kidding with you. I will have my assistant send them out to you, no problem and please, don't pull this type of stunt again. Do ya hear me?"

"Yes, ma'am.   And thanks for understanding." Dexter's voice was a little more relaxed by Vanity's agreeable disposition.

"Understanding? Hell, I was sitting here trying to figure out how I was going to explain these earrings to my husband."

"Oh, yea." Dexter didn't really give much thought to what her husband would think. He just wanted to do something special for his Vanity.

"Yea and I had yet to come up with a good excuse other than the fact that we're mad at each other and I always go shopping, so that was a stretch - we're not that mad at each other."

They both laughed and chatted for a few minutes. He told her that he would be back in a few weeks for the presentation of the campaign and that they should get together for dinner. Vanity tentatively agreed but told him not to pencil her in just yet. She had to clean things up with Winston or she would be looking for a place to live herself. Michelle came in at Vanity's request to get the package to send back to Dexter's office.

For the rest of the afternoon Vanity got a chance to look at some new deals that her associates were presenting. Business was booming and she missed her partner sharing the load. It was a little overwhelming when she realized how many proposals they had to present over the next two weeks.

Before she left the office for the day, she told Michelle to schedule a half day of meetings with the associates so the proposals could be presented to Cole on her first day back. She needed to get in the loop with all the new ideas, as well as distract her from everything at home. On her way out, she received a text from Winston. It said, "Dinner?"

"At home. I am not up for going out," she texted back.

"I thought you would want to get out," he responded.

"It's been a long day. Besides, I have to pick up dry cleaning and go to the drug store for a couple of things."

"I understand. I will see you when you get home." He replied.

When she finally got home, she could tell that the mood was set for something romantic. When she came into the kitchen from the garage, she saw that Winston had dinner on the stove, the sun was setting to the west through the bay windows and jazz music was playing on the surround sound. She thought to herself, this was going to be an interesting night. He wanted sex.

Ever since she and Dexter connected, Winston had not had sex, at least not with Van. She had not so much as desired him for anything of the sort nor had he made any advances to have sex. What had changed? She was not sure what, but she was sure as hell going to find out whether she wanted to or not.

"Wow," she said.

"What? I can't cook dinner for my wife and daughter," Winston said smiling.

"Yea, I am a bit shocked, that's all."

"Well, I figured that whatever is going on with you that a little dinner could help you get through the evening. Besides, Christina's flight this morning was cancelled so she's catching the late flight out this evening."

"I know about the flight. I just wasn't expecting dinner."

Again, with a smile, Winston looked into Van's eyes and said, "Well for what it's worth, I have to eat, too."

At that comment, she knew he got the hint that she was not impressed by the surprised dinner but he remained neutral. She was out of the notion of him at this point. Nothing attracted her to him, not even his late ass attempt at cooking dinner for her. They had spent at least the last five years just mulling around as if they were roommates. The only time they spent together was when it was required; at her work functions or his. Date night? A night on the town...yea, well that hadn't happened in years. They lived in one of the liveliest cities in the world, yet they have the most boring life together. You can't recover from that over a steak dinner.

In the shower, she thought about her daughter, and the fact that she hardly spent any time with her this trip. Christina's friends and social life were a priority as usual and that was fine. The last thing she needed was Chris feeling the vibe between them, so Winston's gesture would be good for her to see. She did not need to see them falling apart in front of her. Her thoughts moved to Dexter. How he had managed to come turn her boring mundane world into excitement. She felt something awaken in her. She felt sexy again. She felt like she was beautiful again. His touch was genuine and he made her comfortable with her love handles. He made her feel things she had not felt in many years or ever. Hell, the last time she could think of Winston making her feel like this was when they first met nearly twenty years ago. Why did it always seem to happen like that? Men stop telling the woman that she is beautiful soon after the bonds of marriage. They must think why bother to impress her. Why is it necessary to keep her excited and interested? She's mine! Did

Dexter treat his wife like that? Was that why he had turned to Vanity for something fresh and new? Vanity began seeing all of these questions before her. Contentment and happiness were what she sought in life from her mate, her work and anything else she put her efforts toward; but she'd be damned if she fell for a guy who would put her on an emotional ride only to push her aside once he got tired and wanted something new. Why did it have to be so damn complicated at this stage in her life? Maybe it was not that hard and she was just making it that way by being stuck in a rut that she had not done anything to get out of. Things had to change and time would sure as hell tell, because Dexter had her full attention. As bad as things could be, it was the fact that he had her in a place where she had wanted to be and that kept her wanting more, regardless of the cost.

At the end of dinner, they got ready to take Christina to the airport. Winston volunteered them both to take her - she knew he was being slick. He wanted to get some time in the car with her on the way home to "talk". He would be in for a rude awakening because she planned to close her eyes and get a little sleep on the way back.

They arrived at the airport within twenty minutes, and kissed their daughter as they sent her off to catch her flight. Christina was comfortable traveling and did not need their escort. As a child, they took family vacations every summer. She had more stamps on her passport then most adults Vanity knew. Christina shared with Vanity that life was not about just school and work, and after graduation, she planned to move to Dubai for a year before coming to work at the firm. They always told their daughter to take her time and see the world before the bonds of a nine to five. Vanity was happy that Christina had the ability to be adventurous and exploratory. Both Vanity and Winston were excited that she decided to take her time building her career, and besides Vanity was nowhere near ready to retire and pass the torch.

"See you guys!" Christina said, as she began grabbing bags to make her rush from the car. .

"Bye, sweetie, call us when you land," said Vanity.

"Yea, yea, I know. I will," she said and kissed them both on the cheek before getting out of the backseat. Knowing that they would still be there, Christina turned around, as she was half way to the automatic doors. As she waved back at her parents, Winston could see the police car inching closer, moving drivers double-parked on, but he refused to move one inch until his baby girl had safely passed through the airport doors.

This was an unspoken feeling that he and Vanity still shared. No matter how grown up, in their hearts Christina was still "their baby girl." As they finally pulled away from curbside, Vanity's phone chirped in her purse. She recognized that it was a text message and had planned to ignore it, but Winston was ready to ask questions. "Aren't you going to answer it?" He asked.

"Answer what?" Vanity replied nonchalantly.

"Your phone. It rang, didn't it?"

Staring out the passenger window, Vanity replied, "It's not a phone call. It's a text message and I will check it later."

Winston was prepared to press the issue, "Why later? It could be important." He asked and stated.

Vanity was prepared as well, but she really did not feel like going through the back and forth, "If it was important, they'd call."

"Are you avoiding looking at it because I am with you?" Winston asked.

"Oh, please Winston, don't start."

"Don't start? You have some nerve!" said Winston.

"Really? What is that supposed to mean?" asked Vanity in a sharp tone.

"You're walking around here acting like you're so upset and going through something, but I think it's only like that around me," he said with conviction.

Winston found a layer of strength that Vanity did not expect, nor even anticipated coming forward...not from him, not in that tone of voice. In all reality, it was mildly attractive to her. Still, she needed to maintain her guard, give him the fight he needed to hopefully stray him away from the source of her "transformation, metamorphosis," change or whatever the hell buzz word he had used to describe just how damn good she felt about herself, about the man that made her feel like a Victoria Secret model.

She responded, "What would give you that idea?"

"I've been watching you and whatever it is you're doing, it makes you glow in the morning." He took the corner hard, as his anger seemed raised.

Now, all of a sudden he had "woman's intuition"! What the hell? She was expecting him to repeat that he had noticed her clothes and hair again but he said she was "glowing". Vanity wanted to smile, she wanted to let out a chuckle at his statement and she did. Both of which seemed to piss Winston off even more. That response from him made her feel even better. Vanity could not deny that he was right, but she could never admit that now, not at this point, especially with the uncertainty of where she and Dexter were going with this "thing" of theirs.

As much as she wanted to be free from Winston, she could not let it end this way, not on terms that she had not created. Besides, he did not deserve all of the blame in this, he really had not done anything wrong, other than be settled in this marriage the same way she did. What Vanity did know was that Dexter came along and sparked a flame; she had been glowing ever since.

"That's ridiculous," she said, still chuckling.

"Vanity, I have known you for twenty years. I know when you're happy, sad and in between. Something or someone has come between us," he said.

In a more controlled manner, Vanity decided it was time to take control of the situation, she said, "We have known each other for a long time and it pains me to know that we've spent a lot of these years just taking each other for granted. You are at the school a lot and I am at the firm a lot. How do you expect things to grow when we don't spend any time together?"

"Is that what this is about? You're acting out because we don't spend time together?" He asked.

"It's more than that," she replied.

That was the final word; they finished the ride in silence. It was as if he was trying to figure it out without asking her. Winston could tell she was being forced to talk. He did not push her for an explanation, and Vanity knew what she meant, even if he didn't.

It was all of the things she said to herself in the shower. It was being tired of this relationship and her deep desire for a change, for excitement, love, lust, and happiness. Was Dexter the change she wanted? For the moment, maybe yes, but overall, it was more than Dexter. It was about her growing and being in a new place in life. Turning forty had not been fun at all. Thoughts about her life came to mind daily, where her life was going, how would her final chapter be written, and with whom. For Vanity, these thoughts did not look so exciting. This was supposed to be the time she was enjoying life and her relationships, but she did not feel joy or even contentment. With all that she had accomplished, all she had gained and earned, she lived in the house she had built from the soil up, she drove expensive cars, traveled at will and she was still unfulfilled. She felt empty and alone. Dexter gave her the excitement in a relationship that she had been missing.

Four

Cole's coming back to the office was refreshing even though her toughest days were still ahead. She seemed to be in a good mood given the circumstances. Vanity and Cole took the morning to catch up on business and planned to take a long lunch to catch up on other things.

Vanity's mood was so-so after speaking with Winston, but she maintained her focus on Cole. Vanity viewed life from the perspective that instead of getting better at it, understanding the ups and downs of life, she had made life even more complicated. Like the roller coaster rides that were once attractions at Coney Island in Brooklyn, New York, she had become the twist and turns. She was life's roller coaster without the stop lever.

Dexter seemed like a great answer to her roller coaster, but Winston filled that same gap at one time, too. The difference between the two of them was simply the way they matured in their lives. Dexter was still exciting and passionate, growing, he lived life without excuses or apologies, and he was sexy as hell. Winston, he just lived life accepting of the things that most people consider constants. He never attempted to be seductive, attractive or otherwise. He was boring. Of the two, Dexter managed to flicker this flame of inner passion, he could make her pussy wet just thinking about him!

****

Vanity decided to reach out to Dexter before lunch to make sure that he received the package that Michelle sent to his office.

"Hi, Ms. Lady," he said.

"Hello Mr. McKnight. Did you receive the package?"

"Yes. Hey, thanks for cleaning up my mess," he said.

"Don't mention it, but we have to be more careful."

"Be more careful? So does this mean that you are not going to fight me anymore? We can continue seeing each other and you won't change your mind on me, on us?" He asked.

"Don't get too comfortable with this."

"Comfortable is what you make me, so why not?" He asked.

"Dexter, we have to be careful about what we're truly asking for. We are risking a lot, including our careers by getting involved."

"You're right, Van. I'm sorry for making it sound comical, or like this is a game." He said.

"Alright, then. Let's keep our business heads. I have no intention of giving up half of my business for you!" she said jokingly, but in a serious tone.

It shocked her that she even thought of the consideration of a divorce, and Winston actually trying to take her for half of her net worth. Now with that thought in the air, she had breathed life into it, gave it existence, suddenly divorce was an option, and scary prospect.

Winston made a very respectable income at the university, but Vanity's income put them in a different tax bracket. Vanity said, "Winston could divorce me and become a multi-millionaire overnight."

Dexter softly replied, "I'm in the same boat with you." The words that filled the air between them created an awkward moment of silence as they wallowed in their own thoughts.

Vanity was not really in a mood to eat and didn't know if Cole was either, but it was the best way for them to get out of the office and have some private time to talk. Vanity played with the idea of telling Cole about Dexter but it didn't seem like something to brag about with anyone, but it was also burning her up inside that, she couldn't share the feelings that she had for him with her best friend.

"You ready?" Vanity said at the threshold of Cole's office.

"Yep. Let me finish this email and I'll be right out," Cole said not looking up from her computer.

VanCole occupied the top floor of a tri-level building. Cole's office sat on the east wing of the building and Vanity's sat on the west. The building was designed for multiple businesses so Van and Cole both wanted a space that would attractive to doctors, lawyers and other small businesses.

Vanity made her way to the elevator where she waited for Cole to join her. While waiting, her phone chirped, it was a text message. "How about dinner tomorrow night?" It was Dexter.

"Tomorrow?" Vanity texted back.

"Yes, tomorrow. I want to see you." He replied.

"You just left last week. You're not due back for at least two weeks," she responded.

"Sounds like a no," he responded with a sad face.

"Tomorrow sounds good. Can't wait."

"See you at six. My flight is already booked." He replied.

"You're a piece of work."

"I know." He said.

The grin on her face must have been too obvious when Cole walked up. "What are you smiling about?"

"Oh, nothing."

"Nothing, my ass!" Cole said.

Vanity smiled and with a chuckle said, "Oh, we're back, aren't we?"

"What?" Cole said.

"You never hold your tongue do you?"

"I've known you too long to be pulling that shit." Cole said.

Jokingly, Vanity said, "I said it was nothing so just let it go."

"Whatever," replied Cole, "Where are we going to eat?"

"We're going to your favorite spot on the strip."

They pulled up to Masala Bay and the valet parked the car. The hotel had the one of the best lunch buffets on the strip. When the hotel was built, its groundbreaking idea to have a beach-like pool was one of their biggest selling points.

As they sat at the table, the waiter brought glasses of water with lemon slices on the side. The buffet was pricey, but they felt it was well worth the expense. Vanity got back to the table first and waited for Cole so they could start together. Cole was always the last one to get to the table and the last one to finish her food.

"So are you going to tell me what has you glowing?" Cole asked.

It was showing more than Vanity thought. Vanity knew it was not going to be good if she kept denying Dexter to her best friend. They shared everything but this was embarrassing and exciting at the same time.

"Cole, I do have a lot going on but so do you. I don't want to talk about me with you still planning the funeral and all."

"Look, I have to get back to my life and some normalcy. Besides, if I don't, I will fall into a depression that I may not come out of for a while. My baby is gone. I have cried, gotten angry, prayed, and cried some more and my baby girl is still gone."

"I'm so sorry."

"I appreciate you Van for giving me space but don't push me out of what's going on with you. I need to get back to how things were so I can be all right with my freakin' sanity! Now what the hell is up with you?" She was serious.

Vanity looked at Cole with embarrassment and said, "I cheated on Winston."

"What? With who?" Cole asked.

Cole did not care about why. She already knew that Van was unhappy with her marriage, but she wanted to know who pushed her over the edge.

"A guy I went to high school with."

"A guy?" She said as if Vanity cheated with some random person.

"Yes, a guy that I went to high school with," she repeated.

"And where did you run into this guy?" Cole asked with a measure of sarcasm.

"Here in Vegas. He was here on business."

"What kind of business is he in?" Cole raised an eyebrow.

"Well..." Vanity was hesitant because this was where she knew Cole would not like the outcome, "He's in the restaurant business and he came to Vegas to meet a marketing firm for expansion."

"Oh, no you didn't!"

"Yes. It is Dexter McKnight from McKnight Enterprises."

"Damn, Van!" Cole yelled out.

"Shhhh! Keep your voice down."

"You are jeopardizing the firm. How could you do something like that?" Cole exclaimed.

"It was supposed to be dinner and catching up for old time sake."

"Yea, it was dinner all right. How the hell did this happen?" Cole asked as she leaned forward.

Vanity replayed the last weeks for Cole, she told Cole every detail, everything about the affair came out as if a fairytale story. Cole sat not eating a drop of food, listening attentively to every word from Van's mouth. She didn't seem to be upset once Van explained how everything happened, and how it had made her feel about herself and her introspection of life. Van even told her that Winston had suspected that something was going on.

"What are you going to do? You can't keep up this affair, you're both married," Cole said.

"I know. And every time I try to get away from this idea or try to stop thinking about him something else happens."

"What do you mean something else happens?"

"He just texted me before lunch and told me that he plans to be in Vegas tomorrow to meet me for dinner?"

"Tomorrow?" Cole asked.

"Yes, and I didn't want to say, no."

"Why not?" Cole asked.

As easy as that question was to ask, Vanity did not have an answer. Vanity did not know why she could not tell him no, or that she did not want to carry on this affair any longer. One side of her liked the thrill and rush that she felt from being in intimate places with a man like Dexter, while the other side of her despised the thought of violating her marriage and this woman she had become.

"I don't know," Vanity replied.

"Well you sure as hell better figure it out because this is dangerous. It is not good for you or the firm." Cole said.

Vanity knew Cole was right. She had to get over herself and do what was best.

As they finished lunch, Cole, who had half eaten said, "Girl, I'm not judging you. Hell, you know what's in my closet. However, I'm telling you that this thing will either tear you and your household apart, or it will break your heart. It's up to you to decide your poison. No matter what, I will always be in your corner as your number one 'you go girl' cheerleader and most importantly, your friend."

These words gave Van a sense of stability and reassured her why Cole had been her best friend all these years. What Vanity thought would be a nice lunch to catch up on business turned out to be about her and Dexter.

****

They made it back to the office in plenty of time to get on a conference call with the McKnight firm to discuss the campaign and the upcoming visit. Vanity hoped that Cole was able to keep her attitude in check because she knew how she could be when she was not feeling something.

"Good afternoon," Vanity greeted.

"Good afternoon," Everyone else chimed in.

"Thank you for joining us for this briefing. You all know my partner Nicole; she is joining us on this call today."

"Hi, Nicole, it is great to hear you're back," Dexter's voice came through the speaker.

"Thank you Mr. McKnight. I hear a lot has been accomplished while I've been out, so let's get started," Cole responded.

If no one else could tell, Vanity knew what she meant by "a lot" and it wasn't to insinuate business. Vanity shook her head and thought this would be an interesting partnership from now until completion. Cole was not excited about the turn of events and it was obvious.

"Yes. Let's get started." Dexter confirmed.

At that point, everyone was able to log into the virtual presentation and follow along with the briefing. Vanity handled the details even though Cole came up to speed quickly. The conference call lasted a good hour with the closing about the clients return to Vegas for the groundbreaking at their new location in two weeks.

"Sounds good. I look forward to meeting all of you," Cole concluded.

As the call ended, Vanity dialed Cole's extension. "You are a trip!"

"What?" Cole questioned.

"A lot has been accomplished?" she teased.

"That is what I meant. I was talking about business." Cole said flatly.

"Yea, sure you were."

"I was not insinuating that you two have been carrying on like two little teenagers...if that is what you mean." Cole exclaimed.

"That's exactly what you meant!" she laughed.

"Van, this is not funny." Cole said in a scolding tone.

"I know Cole. I know it's wrong but it feels good to me when I'm doing it and this excitement is what I've been craving for years."

"Damn, girl. You couldn't find this excitement in a single guy, a vibrator, a thick black dildo or something!" Cole said half joking.

"Girl, please! Vegas is not where you want to pick up a guy, and I have toys, I needed arms and legs and...well, I was in need...shit!" Vanity managed a chuckle.

"Yea, I know right!" Even Cole had to laugh at that.

"I'm going to dinner with Dexter tomorrow and try to figure out how to get myself out of this again."

"And he better not pull back on this deal because you stop giving up the goods!" Cole snapped.

"He wouldn't do that. He's a real business man."

"Well, be prepared, if he wants you, he could try and manipulate his way in, now that he thinks he has you where he wants you." Cole said.

"Cole, he isn't like that. Dexter wouldn't do that to me."

"Okay. Don't put anything past him. He is a man with, I guess, good dick."

Van laughed, and said, "Yes lord, and a skilled tongue."

They changed the subject to business but Vanity's mind did wonder back to the conversation that Dexter could try to manipulate her into a relationship to keep him as a client. She could not accept the thought that he would do that. Nonetheless, people were capable of anything devious, so it wouldn't be wise to dismiss the idea all together. Now she felt like she had to keep her eyes open for signs but she hated that Cole put those thoughts in her head in the first place. Vanity was having fun with Dexter in her mind, now this. Her thoughts were tainted with the ideas that he may use her to stay in this affair to keep him satisfied.

****

By 5 o'clock the next afternoon, Vanity was packing up her things to leave for dinner with Dexter. She had told Michelle to let anyone who called know that she was in meetings the rest of the afternoon and to take messages versus sending any to her cell phone. No sooner than she gave that message to her assistant and headed for the elevator, Michelle nearly knocked her down to hand her the message that said that Winston had called and was on his way over to the office to take her out to dinner.

"What the hell for?" She said aloud, as she took the message from Michelle. "Thank you Michelle, I'll call him."

She dug her phone from her purse immediately to catch him before he made it halfway. She needed him to know that she had a dinner meeting already planned with a client and that she had no intention to cancel.

When she called his phone, it went directly to voicemail. He was in either a dead zone or avoiding her calls so she couldn't cancel. He pulled this stunt once before trying to make up for something, but it would not work this time either. When she made it to her car, she saw that Winston's car was in the parking lot. They must have just missed each other on the elevator.

Positive that he saw her car in the parking lot, she only had a few minutes to get moving before he came out after her. She could hear Michelle now telling him that he just missed her. There was no going back, she was on a mission and she was not in the mood to sit across the table from Winston.

As she made it to the main drag, her phone was doing its ringing thing. "Hello," she answered.

It was Winston, he said "Vanity, where are you going?"

"What do you mean, where am I going?"

"Yes. Didn't you get my message?" He asked.

"I did get the last minute message you left with Michelle."

"You were just here. I saw your car." He said.

"I was on my way out. I tried to call you but your voicemail picked up. I have a meeting that I had on the calendar for the past week or so. I couldn't cancel just because you want to surprise me for dinner all of a sudden."

"A dinner meeting?" He asked.

"Yes, a dinner meeting, so I am sorry that your timing is off but I am on my way there now and I will be home later."

The call disconnected. Vanity looked at the phone surprised, "Hello?"

He was obviously pissed. He must have hung up the phone but she did not bother to call him back.

She made it to the Cosmo hotel and quickly made her way to the restaurant. In sight of the host station, she saw Dexter standing at the entrance in a pair of jeans and a button down shirt. He did not see her approaching so she was able to get a full glimpse of him looking off into the crowd. She exhaled making a mental note of how good he looked and made her feel. She could not believe this man wanted to see her. Her stride must have become obvious along with heels that were tapping the marble floors, as he turned and saw her. "Hi, babe." He leaned in for a kiss when she approached.

"Hi," she said but her voice cracked.

"Are you okay? You look frazzled." He asked.

"I am. My husband just got me a little off beat," she cleared her throat.

"What happened?" He asked.

"Let's not talk about that right now. Let's eat."

"Ok, if you say so. I am down with that." He said.

The hotel was busy as usual. It wasn't one of Vanity's usual spots, and the name alone attracted young and progressive visitors. To get a little less of the crowd, the table was off in a corner of the restaurant where they could talk about anything and no one would hear them. Vanity felt her phone buzzing on the way to the table. She took it from her purse just to see who it was, Winston. She stopped short of the table and excused herself to take the call.

"Hello?" She responded in a whisper and with clear irritation in her tone.

"Are you at your meeting yet?" Winston questioned.

"Yes, and I am being rude taking your call. What is it now?"

"I want to talk when you get home." Winston stated admittedly.

"Is that it? You could have told me that earlier before you hung up on me. I have to go."

It was rude to talk to her husband in that tone but for some reason, she had grown frustrated with Winston and really had no desire to "talk". Based on the past five years, they did not make talking a priority. At this point, she was not interested.

"Okay, I will be waiting up." He replied.

"Fine," she said and hung up the phone.

Dexter was waiting on her to end her call so he could pull out her chair before seating himself. He did not ask about the call and she did not tell. She was not in the mood to talk about Winston, especially not with Dexter. The server took their drink orders of which Dexter ordered their usual, Beefeater and ginger ale.

"So, how did you get out of the earring deal?" Vanity started the conversation.

"Oh, I told her that they were sent to a client by mistake." Dexter replied.

"She bought that?"

"Yea, she was just happy to wear them. I haven't bought her anything like that in years. Now my problem is that she thinks that we're rekindling our marriage because of that gift," He said in a very disinterested manner.

"Oh, how so?"

"She's been dressing differently and trying to get my attention and she wants to have sex," Dexter proclaimed.

"Sex? And how are you handling that?"

"I have to be honest with you. I have to play along so she doesn't suspect anything?"

As that piece of revelation left Dexter's lips, suddenly he looked guilty. As if, he was cheating on Vanity with his wife.

"So, in other words, you're having sex."

"Well, yea. I don't want to, but I have to," he said.

This conversation was no better than talking about Winston. She did not want to hear about Dexter having sex with his wife. She had no desire to be with Winston like that, no matter what type of ice he flashed at her.

"Let's talk about something else," she blurted.

"Good idea," he agreed.

The drinks came and the conversation switched to business. That was something that they both could talk about without mentioning their significant other. They talked about other client business and ventures they were tackling as CEOs. Vanity thought about how good it felt to talk to someone about business other than Cole. Winston was never interested in her business and her impact on the Vegas nightlife. The only time he was interested was when she got freebies of which he could partake. It was common for them to travel and stay at resorts free, go to concerts and shows at the hotels. Although she still received the benefits, she had stopped sharing them with Winston a long time ago. Out of the blue, the conversation became about them again.

Dexter said, "Are you able to spend the night with me?"

Vanity was about to answer but was distracted by the server near the front of the restaurant pointing towards them. Then the server started walking toward their table. He had something in his hand and she could not make out what it was.

"A message for you ma'am," the server handed Vanity a restaurant bar napkin.

"A message?" Dexter asked leaning back in his chair, as he quickly scanned the room.

She did not want to open it. It could not be good news, not like this. She opened the note and read it:

"I know your dirty little secret. End it now." It read.

No signature but the handwriting was obvious to her. It was Winston. She would have wondered how he found her, but there were very few yellow Maserati's with pearl colored leather interior on the Vegas strip, the hotels and restaurants loved parking exotic cars in the front where everyone could see them. All Winston had to do was drive by a few hotels and he would find her. She just did not think he would go to such lengths.

"Well?" Dexter looked puzzled.

"It was my husband," Vanity replied in a shallow voice.

"What? How?" Dexter was on high alert, and repositioned himself to gain a better view of the entire dining area.

"I assume he drove down the strip to see if he saw my car. I guess he was successful."

"He's following you." This was more of a statement than a question.

Vanity tried to remain calm because if she knew Winston, he had made his point, and had gone home.

He was not into making a scene. It was going to be a long night, she thought.

"Dexter, this has to end."

"We can't stop just like that," said Dexter.

"Dexter," she said with annoyance in her tone. "He knows about us. This has gone too far."

"Calm down Vanity." He said, taking her hand into his.

"Let's go."

"We haven't eaten." Dexter responded as he sat back.

"Eat? I can't eat right now. My stomach is in knots. I need to go."

She started gathering her purse and waved for the server to bring over the check.

"Yes, ma'am?" he asked as he approached the table.

"Please bring the check."

"Ma'am, your meal has not been served," the server said.

"Yes, I know. That's okay, I will handle the bill," she said trying to rush him.

"Would you like your meal to go?"

"Fine! Just bring the damn check, please!"

Vanity had grown irritated in that very short period. What was she going to do? It was not supposed to happen like this. She was supposed to enjoy a little fun, and it would end and no one would find out.

"Vanity, please calm down." Dexter took her shaking hands and somehow absorbed all the weird energy from her body. She closed her eyes, as they welled up with tears that fell as soon as she opened them. This man sitting across the table had a way of making her feel all right. The heat from her anger slowly returned to a normal temperature. The server had brought the bill and the doggie bags to the table. Dexter's right hand reached for his wallet to pay the bill, while his left secured Vanity's hand.

"Please come up with me for a while," he said.

She wasn't going to fight it, didn't have the strength to say no, in reality, if Vanity left now, she would be going home to face the truth, to face Winston and she was not ready for that.

"Okay." Vanity answered in a defeated tone.

As they exited the restaurant, and made their way through the lobby towards the elevators, she did not attempt to look around for Winston. Dexter did, he stayed ever vigilant with a heightened sense of awareness about him. Vanity on the other hand knew Winston would not be anywhere in the immediate vicinity. That type of thing was not the man Winston was. Dexter took her arm in his and boldly walked with her as if she was his wife. He held her as though they belonged together. She felt like she belonged to him, was a part of him, they were together. Her marriage was over and she had driven a stake in it by wanting to be with Dexter even the more. What did he have on her? Why was she so willing to let years of marriage go just to be with him. Safely in the elevator, encapsulated by the four walls, he turned and lifted her chin to meet him for a sensual kiss. It sent shock waves through her body, right down to her clit. He excited her. He had awakened her. That's what he did that to her. Dexter breathed life into her existence. That is what had her in this place. He did something to the core of her, something that she had not felt before. Somehow, he knew exactly what her body needed. Her sexuality had been dormant and she did not want to go back to that feeling ever again. The elevator stopped on the Penthouse floor. Inside the room, instead of taking her to the bed and ripping her clothes off, he went to the Jacuzzi.

"We're going to unwind," he demanded.

Her silence was agreement. He ran the Jacuzzi while she undressed. No matter what he had in mind, she was going along with it. The room was cozy and he turned the lights down as they got into the bubbling water. With just enough light shining in from the Vegas Strip, the ambience was perfect.

"Vanity I want you to relax." He turned on very soft music, mellow jazz, before he sat across from her. Gently lifting her leg, his hands slowly, trickled down to her feet; he rubbed and massaged her toes and the soles of her feet. Dexter took each leg, rubbing the tension away, going higher into her inner thigh while occasionally caressing her clit. He took her hands and massaged them, her arms, and her breast. He did not make a sound. He let the music play and his hands did all the talking. He was connecting with her body. He did all he could to keep her mind relaxed. Her thoughts about what would happen later were dissolving; she had let her mind go to another place. He pulled her over to him and she sat between his legs. He hummed to the instrumental sound of Maxwell, one of his favorite songs, as he massaged her shoulders and kissed the back of her neck. If there had been any tension left in her body, it was gone.

"Let's make love," she broke the silence.

No words spoken, Dexter stood and grabbed the towels from the hook and stepped out of the tub. His manhood was ready and willing to fulfill her command. His body still dripping water, glistening in the dim light, ghostly, yet defining every inch of him. Dexter reached for her hand to help her out of the tub and gently dried her off. He came prepared for this moment. He grabbed a bottle of oil from the basin counter and massaged it into her damp body. She was in heaven. Dexter guided her to the bed and pulled back the comforters.

Vanity said, "It's my turn to give you something in return for all you've given me."

Dexter smiled and allowed Vanity to take control. She lay on top of him, her breast massaged his hairy chest and stomach; her tongue explored his lips and neck. She wanted to drink him in, pleasure him as he had pleasured her time after time. Vanity nipples were hard and tingled as they crossed Dexter's chest, but it was her tongue, her lips that she wanted to give him. She was licking and sucking everywhere. Dexter's nipples were sensitive to her touch, she realized this as his muscles contracted when her tongue and mouth licked and sucked on him. With his nipple in her mouth, on her tongue, her hand found his dick, hard and thick, she stroked it. Dexter's stomach caved in as Vanity found the right rhythm between dick stroking and nipple sucking. She did not want him to nut yet, she made sure he would not, she wanted to tease his cum, she wanted his toes to crack and hear him call her name. Vanity's tongue game would prove to be her weapon of choice. She ran her lips from his nipple down his stomach, and with a swift move, without missing a stroke of his cock, her lips spread open to his throbbing dick, she sucked it wet and long. Feeling the veins pulsating on her tongue made her pussy wetter, as she knew that he would soon release for her, she would have him, and she could taste him. Vanity ran her tongue the length of his shaft to his balls and her lips opened to receive them, her tongue played right between his long dick and smooth balls. This motion thrilled Dexter, gave his dick fits and made him lose control of this thigh muscle.

He said, "Damn.....damn, do that shit girl!"

For minutes Vanity stayed there, manipulating Dexter's prostate while stroking his dick, which proved to be fun to her, enjoyable, for she was firmly in control and she did like control. When it became apparent from the throbbing of his dick he was about cum, Van ran her tongue up the shaft to the head, kissing and sucking all the way up. Her lips took him in, as her tongue found a spot to claim. Dexter clutched the sheets. Blood left his brain. Van sucked hard, and harder, as she attempted to pull the seed out of him. Dex's dick throbbed and he could feel his release pushing, begging to get out. Van held the base of his cock, firmly. With one finger, she massaged his prostate, with her mouth; she coated the head of his dick, kept it wet, tongue still in that one spot.

Dexter screamed out, "OH SHIT..." He was coming, in her mouth, on her lips, as if he held this build up for this moment, for her. She was pleased to show him that skills were not one sided. What he gave to her she could give back to him. She tasted him, she swallowed him, and she enjoyed doing this for him. Dexter shivered and spasms ran through him. His brain swayed black with flashes of red, green...colors. He regained his senses and took Van into his arms. He stared into her eyes, and then proceeded to mount her. Sucking her neck, his lips kissing her breast, his tongue flicking at her nipples, he licked and kissed her stomach. Dexter spread her thighs with a push from his broad shoulders, he spread her pussy with his soft lips and found her wetness, in his mind he could hear her pussy beg, "Dex, eat from me, feed from me, lick me," and he did. His tongue flicked Vanity's clit as two fingers entered her wet soft pussy to find her g-spot. Dex massaged this spot as Vanity's hips danced; grinding her fat wet pussy into his face. Her juice dripped on his chin, ran down her ass, and his tongue flicked her clit repeatedly. She was getting an oral bath. The faster his tongue moved, the more he increased gentle pressure to her g-spot with the tips of his fingers. Van could feel the sparks, the tingle coursing through her pelvis, the electricity surging through her stomach, almost astounding her, taking her breath away. She grabbed his head as her body began to explode, she had lost control, he was taking her with his tongue and fingers, making her cum with his mouth.

As she grinded her wetness in his face, she said, "Is this what you want? You want me to cum on your face. You want me to fuck your lips, fuck your face...oh god, yes eat this pussy, baby..." Her orgasm was from somewhere deep, thick flowing juice squirted forward. Her body went into multiple spasms as she finally was forced to slap at Dex, begging him to stop, her heart felt as if it was going to drop, ready to stop. "Ohhhhh, please no, yessss, please ohhhh. Dammit, I can't take it...stop!" Dexter pleased her, kissing her lips. Then he eased his body off Vanity long enough to push her on her side. Standing firmly on the carpet, knees bent and dick ready again, he entered her, stroked her from a side angle. She could feel all of him deep in her, all of him rubbing the tip of her g-spot, the walls of her juicy pussy. His strong hands grabbed her ass and spread her cheeks apart, so every stroke was as if she was double penetrated, "Dammmmn," she enjoyed it. Her pussy cheered with more juice coating his long thick dick. She could hear her juice as he stroked her, she could smell their sex...it was erotic and she came again. Van's pussy muscles grabbed Dexter's dick as if to milk it, she matched every stroke he gave and when she twisted her hips and let her lady muscle whip, he moaned. She felt full of electricity and without any effort, her body exploded with another orgasm that gushed from her pussy. Her body was out of control and his long stroke caused the orgasm to continue. Dexter could no longer hold back, the overflow of wetness coming from her pussy was too much for him to resist, Dexter let out a groan she had not heard from him before. He kept his strokes long throughout his orgasm; she turned and looked up at him, stared on his face as the grimace slowly faded. He leaned forward and kissed her.

"Damn, I love you," he said.

"I love you, too," she replied.

They didn't speak any other words. He got back on the bed next to Van and their breathing eventually became normal after a few minutes and before long, they were sleeping.

****

"Van, wake up."

She jumped up and realized she was still in the hotel, "Oh my god! What time is it?"

"It's 9."He said.

"Oh, I have to get home," she said.

"I know. I wanted to let you sleep but I know you have to go." He replied sadly.

"Yes, I wish things were different but I have to go home and face a little reality." She said calmly.

"I am sorry it happened this way but I am not sorry for being in love with you Vanity." Dexter confessed.

"Yea, well I wish we were free to love openly. I don't like sneaking around and I wanted those damn Tiffany diamonds!" she said, with a grin.

"Oh, that's what you want? I will have them to you soon... "

"Of course, I wanted the gift. It's just, I was afraid of getting caught with them but hey, the cat is out of the bag now."

"Yea, well only on your end. I still have to tread lightly," said Dexter, in an unsure voice.

"I know but we'll have to lay low too so I can clear things up. Winston is probably going to want to go to counseling." She said shaking her head.

"Just comply to keep the peace and if you're ready to walk away from the marriage, I will be here to support you." Dexter grinned.

"I bet you will," she said, jabbing his muscular forearm.

After her quick shower and getting dressed, she pulled her hair back into the ponytail it was in and made her way to the door. Dexter was right on her heels. She could tell he did not want her to go but she had to go face Winston. She was preparing herself for an argument so she had to snap out of this lovey dovey phase.

"OK. I'll call you tomorrow, baby," she said quickly.

"Please do." He kissed her and she opened the door and was off to face the music.

Five

Vanity pulled into the driveway, the motion censored lights lit up the pathway to the garage. She pressed the door opener from the visor and as expected Winston's car was in its usual spot. She pulled in and turned off the ignition. She sat in the car a few moments to gather her thoughts, hoping the tongue-lashing was not going to be too bad. She entered through the kitchen and saw the library light still on. It was quiet but she knew he was still up. She dropped her keys and purse on the table and went to the fridge to grab a bottle of water and when she closed the door, there he was. He had a look in his eyes that she had never seen before.

Startled by his presence, "You scared me," she said.

"Who is he?" He asked.

She thought about a quick answer then she realized that he had not witnessed her cheating but only having dinner with a man. It still could have been business since that is where she said she was going. She could still deny this affair. Hell, she had been lying all this time. What's one more that he can't actually prove, since he never saw them in the act?

"Winston, you're overreacting. Why are you following me around?"

"Overreacting!" He started to raise his voice.

"Yes. I told you I had a meeting."

"It looked a little more intimate than that." He said.

"Dexter McKnight is a new client, if you must know. It was a planned meeting. I don't know why you sent such a message to the table. It was so embarrassing."

Frustration in his eyes, he said, "Okay, Vanity. You must think I am a fool."

Vanity stepped back from the fridge and leaned against the sink counter, "I told you, nothing happened."

"Why are you lying? You have been acting different for weeks, and I finally see you with another man and you think I didn't notice how you two were looking at each other? He may be a client but he's more than that and you know it!" Winston shouted.

"Look, I told you it was nothing. So, just drop it," she said sounding annoyed by his accusations. Inside she was in knots. The perfect opportunity to come clean and she blew it. She had to ride this lie out to the end. Winston didn't believe it, he was not buying her acting job this time, she felt and saw it in his eyes, she had to push back; things were just too close for comfort.

"Drop it? I will do no such thing. We have problems and we need to fix them or this isn't going to work any longer Vanity." He said.

"Problems, oh, it's only been years since you've been anywhere near interested in what I have going on in my life, let alone treat me like you're still attracted to me. Problems, we have problems but don't try to pretend like I've changed all of a sudden, and now we have problems," she said in a matter of fact manner.

"Fine. I will give you that but that doesn't mean we just give up and start having affairs," said Winston.

"Affairs? Stop it, OK! I have tried to make things better over the years and I am just tired. You see someone or so you think, showing me interest and now you want to step up. Believe me Winston; I get more of a spark from my toys than you have been able or even desired to give me in years."

"What's that supposed to mean?" Winston asked.

Sucking her teeth, Vanity made a smack with her lips and stormed off. She made her way up to her master bathroom so she could get ready for a shower, but heard Winston behind her. She hurried to get into the bathroom before he got up there. Knocking on the door, in a more controlled voice Winston said, "Vanity, open the door."

"I don't want to talk about this anymore. I'm going to take a shower and get ready for bed; I've had a long day."

"Fine, but we're not finished. I want us to resolve this. I looked online for a counselor and made an appointment," he said before walking away.

"Great," she said dreadfully under her breathe.

In the shower, she drifted her thoughts to Dexter. He told her he loved her tonight. She inhaled the steam from the shower and it was as if she could smell the masculine scent of his cologne in the air. Her nipples were immediately aroused. She took each breast in her hands and gave them a gentle squeeze to satisfy their desire. Eyes still closed, visions of Dexter caused her clit to ache for attention, she had to respond, she wanted to seek out her own pleasure. Vanity gave her clit a gentle rub. With one leg up on the ledge of the full size shower, she put more emphasis on her clit and within minutes, those rubs became rapid circular motions creating a nice release. She exhaled to feel the fullness of her orgasm. It was at that moment she realized that her sex drive was increasing. Why, she asked herself. Why was she feeling horny at the strangest times? She ignored her own question to give herself more. By the time she finished, she had been in the shower nearly twenty minutes. She stood under the running water, head tilted back, running her fingers through her hair. She felt sexy and Dexter helped her feel this way.

She smiled and whispered, "Damn, I love that man."

****

For the next two weeks, Dexter and Vanity laid low. Even though business for him was picking up in Vegas, they kept their visits during business hours and occasionally mid-day lunch dates for a little passionate fun. Cole was back on her regular schedule after the funeral. She started taking over the McKnight project slowly but confidently. Cole and Dexter had become better acquainted and other than the fact that Dexter was fucking her best friend, for which she was not happy about, she began to admire the man.

This day was to be the first counseling session that Winston set up for them. He wanted to give Vanity enough notice to plan it into her schedule. She was not thrilled about it, but she figured to keep the peace and get some things out in the open, it couldn't hurt to go. When she pulled into the parking lot, she saw that Winston had already arrived. He was probably waiting impatiently inside since she was fashionably late.

On her way out of the car, Vanity made a quick call to Cole to see if she was out of her meeting. Cole updated her on the latest project and told Van that the McKnight Firm would be back in Vegas in a few days. Vanity downplayed that part, attempting to be nonchalant, not giving any real attention to seeing Dexter. Besides, she already knew about his upcoming visit. Cole didn't agree with the affair, and was still bothered and put off by it. She thought that Vanity was ruining a good marriage and Dexter was just a fling that would never amount to anything-long term. Cole was probably right on both fronts, but Cole was not dealing with what Van had to deal with in her marriage. Cole had always been happy and progressive in her marriage despite the challenges with having a child. She and Robert spent lots of time together, did things with each other and for each other. It was always the little things that made Vanity envious of the relationship that they had. Along with the many vacations, he surprised Cole with; he was sensitive to Cole's needs. He would come to the office with their bags already packed and whisk her off to Paris or Brazil or some other exotic place. Of course, Van had to help him work that out by making sure she cleared Cole's calendar for the time they would be gone and fluff her schedule to make her look busy, but that's the kind of relationship they had. That was the kind of relationship Vanity wanted but Winston had never planned anything like that for them. If Vanity did not plan it, send him a calendar reminder listing the date, time and location, they didn't go. The reality was their marriage had run its course and she was ready to do more things in life and since Winston was happy-go-lucky as is, she just could not, and would not live like that another twenty years. Life had too much to offer and was short as hell so she wanted to enjoy it, and her empty nest.

She entered the counselor's office and saw Winston sitting in the corner chair reading a magazine. He didn't look up when she came through the door so she went to the receptionist to let her know that they were both ready.

The receptionist gave her a clipboard and some documents to sign and told her that the doctor would be with them shortly. Vanity sat one seat away from Winston, putting her purse in that vacant seat between them. He finally looked up.

"Glad you could finally make it," he said with an attitude about her tardiness.

Ignoring his comment, she finished the paperwork. When she had completed signing her life away and telling all of her damn business, the counselor was ready for them.

The office, for as large as it was, was nice and cozy. It was typical - a worn leather sofa, dark cherry wood furniture and a bookshelf full of titles. Her accolades were hanging on every wall along with some dull artwork in between. She was a Caucasian woman with a slim build. She stood tall and her face was old and stressed looking. Vanity noticed her wedding band, which looked about as old as she was. She shook her head and thought to herself, "I hope he only paid for an hour of this shit."

The session lasted a little over an hour and by the time it was over, they were no better off than they were before. At least that is what Vanity thought. The counselor told them that they needed to come back individually to discuss what they needed to work on, but Vanity had no interest in that. She was ready to get her ass out of there. They had spent the entire time focusing on what Winston told the counselor, which of course were his suspicions. Vanity still had no intentions on spilling the beans, but she let him air his concerns. In her own defense, she told the counselor what she had already told Winston. They were growing apart and that was just the way it was. The counselor gave them some homework to do and told them to bring back results for the next meeting. They had to think about what made them fall in love in the beginning and reenact one of those moments or events. The idea was to spark something in them that they could both relate to. Vanity rolled her eyes when she heard the homework assignment.

Winston was setting up the next appointment as Vanity walked out. Vanity got to the car not giving time for Winston to catch up. She had another meeting to get to anyway. The winter season was settling in and business was picking up for spring marketing campaigns. She had several deals on her desk to work on. Within twenty minutes, she was back at her desk on the phone with a potential client. This was her element, on the phone negotiating contracts, making deals. Thoughts of the counseling session, needless to say the homework assigned, were far from her thoughts.

By six o'clock Cole stepped into her office and made herself comfortable while she finished her last call. Vanity could see she was anxious to see how the counseling session went but Van was in no mood to talk about that. While trying to wrap up the call Van's phone chirped. It was a message from Dexter,

"How was the meeting?" He asked.

Van thought, "Oh, boy not him, too."

She would satisfy Coles' curiosity first, and then she planned to call Dexter.

"Okay, Cole," she said hanging up the phone.

"So?" Cole said looking at Vanity crazy.

"So, what?" she acted unsure of what she wanted to know.

"Don't play with me Van. How was the counseling? Did you guys get anything accomplished?" Cole questioned.

"It depends on who you ask," said Van.

"What's that supposed to mean?" asked Cole.

"It means what I said. I did not see the point before and definitely not now. It was just a lot of what we've already discussed. Winston needs to wake up. We have grown so far apart that he does not even recognize it. So he thinks that we can talk to a counselor and make it all better."

"Well, you have to try. This thing with Dexter does not make it any better. I told you Van, I don't like it and you need to stop seeing him," Cole said with concern in her voice.

"I hear you, but my marriage was a problem well before Dexter. Winston just happens to notice it now that I am putting more emphasis on other things, like how I look," she said.

"Maybe that's one of the things that you did wrong," Cole said seriously, but it sounded like a joke.

"Oh, please. I am not falling short in the fashion department but I think he just noticed the effort more than anything." Van responded.

"Yea, you're right. You are the only person I know who buys $500 shoes and only wears them once." Cole smiled as she held up a finger and twisted her neck.

"The counselor gave us homework, can you believe it?"

"Oh, yea. What kind of homework?" Cole asked.

"I have to do something I used to do when we were first married or something new to rekindle the flame."

"That's a great idea," Cole exclaimed.

"For who? I don't have time for that right now. Besides, I cannot remember that far back and Winston ain't getting a blow job from me!" They both laughed. It was a good break to the tension in the room.

"Well, you better put some effort into this or you're going to find yourself alone," said Cole.

"Gee, thanks."

"You're the one playing with fire," Cole said.

"Fire? I didn't plan this but to be honest this is the best I have felt in years. This feeling is not so easy to give up. I feel alive. My body feels alive and sadly my husband didn't create this feeling and to let that go, well it's easier said than done," Vanity said.

"I cannot say I understand what you're going through, because I don't..." Cole started.

"You're right. You don't. Your marriage has not suffered the way mine has," Van interrupted.

"Hey, wait a minute. We have our problems too, but we use them to help us grow." Cole clarified.

"Not all couples can do that Cole."

"Okay, I won't press you on this but remember what I said about how this can turn badly." Cole tried to emphasis.

"I will remember and I will continue to keep you out of it because I know you don't approve. You're my friend and business partner, I won't compromise either relationship."

"Damn right! I love you and no, I don't approve, but you're my best friend and I will not let a man come between us so, do you and if you need me, I'm here." Cole said as she came behind Van's desk for a girly girl hug.

By the time they left the office after catching up on what deals they were working on, it was past eight. A call to Dexter was still on the list of things to do. Even though she wasn't in the mood, she knew it was only delaying the inevitable but she just couldn't do it. For some reason Van felt tired, and calling Dexter right now, well she wasn't sure how she felt about that. On top of it all, Cole had drained the last bit of energy she had to talk about the drama in her life.

Vanity drove straight home and decided to send Dexter a text message, "I am home. We will catch up tomorrow. Long day." She sent the text and got out of the car before waiting for a response. All she wanted to do was shower and get in bed.

She made it to the kitchen only to find the lights dim, candles lit and smooth rhythm and blues playing softly in the background. The kitchen table had no food on it, merely a box and card in the center of a platter. She thought, immediately, this was not something they used to do and she sure as hell was not in the mood, but there was nowhere for her to escape, there was nothing else she could do but see where this was going to lead. When she opened the box from Nancy Meyer, her favorite lingerie boutique, inside was a sexy two-piece panty and bra set with a matching cover up, her style.

The card simply said, "Try it on."

Totally caught off guard, she took the box into the in-law suite on the first floor and tried on the set. It was a perfect fit. She didn't even get a chance to leave the room before Winton showed up in his Trilogy Leisurewear, a high end men's boutique on the Vegas strip. In his hand, he held a bottle of wine and flute glasses. He changed the linen in the room and on the bed was pleasure toys and body oils; something else she didn't recall ever happening back when they met. He was definitely on to something new. He hated sex toys. He placed the flutes on the nightstand and poured the two glasses of wine. He took one and handed it to her and then one for himself.

"Have a seat on the bed. I have something to tell you." Winston said.

Vanity sat on the edge of the bed and Winston got down on one knee directly in front of her. "Vanity, I still love you. I am sorry that I have neglected you for so long and I understand if my actions have put you in a crazy place, emotionally. But I'll be damned if I let you walk out of my life without a fight." He was sincere and the look in his eyes said he wanted to try.

Vanity did not mutter a word. She could not believe that Winston had confessed and told her all she had wanted to hear after so long. The last time he had done anything this special, it had been many moons ago. He was not the romantic type but someone must have given him a lesson or two because Vanity was in awe.

"Winston, this is so..." she started.

"I know. And I want you to know that I want you back." He said.

"But I am here." Vanity said.

"No, I mean back, emotionally and physically." He was asking for her love.

"But..." She started but Winston did not let the rest of her words meet the air. He came in for a passionate kiss, nearly spilling the glass of wine she held in her hand. He sat his glass on the nightstand, and grabbed her head for security and kissed her with all the passion within him. While her mind was trying to catch up to what was happening, her body had already responded. She matched his passion and deep tongue kiss to the tee. He took her glass, and put it on the nightstand and laid her back on the bed. He started with another kiss on her lips and moved ear to ear and cheek to cheek. All she could do was close her eyes and enjoy the touch of her husband. He took her breast in his hand and rubbed her soft nipples that were already erect from his touch. He lifted her breast from the cup of her bra and licked it gently, nibbling on her nipple. Vanity was moistening by the second and because of her moans, Winston took his free hand to touch inside her wet thighs. His dick stiffened, and Vanity felt it rub against her thigh and down her leg as he made his way downtown. Instead of taking off the sexy lace panties, he spread her legs to get access where her pussy was already calling.

He took her clit into his mouth. He sucked it gently, teasing it slightly and her juices began to flow from her body into his thirsty mouth. Vanity took him by the head and ran her finger through is wavy hair that gave Winston the clue that he needed to go deeper. Within minutes, Vanity was exploding in his mouth. He stayed there licking and nibbling a little longer giving her multiple orgasms. Her body was shaking and quivering beyond her control. He reached up to slide the panties off as he took control of her body, and he made his way into her. He held onto his wife as if it was their first night. His strokes, deep and slow which caused another explosion in her. Vanity's climax forced Winston out as it overflowed.

"What was that?" Winston asked after Vanity calmed down.

"I don't know. I've never had that happen." Vanity lied. She knew that Dexter was able to make her pussy squirt but all she could do was play along and let Winston feel like the man that he was trying to be.

"I know. It got all over me," Winston said still unsure of what just happened to his wife.

"I need something to drink," she said clearing her parched throat.

Winston reached over to the nightstand where he left the two glasses. He handed Vanity a glass and took his as well. Before he let her take a drink. He grabbed her hand and looked into her eyes. She looked into his eyes not sure of what he wanted to say. Did he want to fight for her? He did not say anything, but she knew it, she felt it. He tapped her glass in a toast as their eyes locked in agreement. She took a sip of her wine and so did he. After a few more sips, she sat the glass back on the nightstand. Vanity took an assessment of her husband who had not let his body go as she had. He was still slender and he still had a six-pack and always kept his facial hair nice and tapered.   Her husband was handsome, sexy even.

Vanity never said her husband was not attractive anymore to her, but over the years, her disinterest made him unattractive. It was funny how the mind could tell the heart exactly what to do. Vanity had convinced herself that she did not want this man touching her anymore and that the only thing he was good for was helping her maintain her lifestyle and that was it. They had nothing in common. They did not talk about their dreams or plans after Christina had grown up, and because of this distance, Vanity had become accustomed to not having sex with him.

After the sex, she saw him in a different light. Just like that the wall that she had up in front of him crumbled. He sat in silence while Vanity was doing her assessment not sure of what she was thinking. She knew he was still unsure of where she stood, but when she gave him a nibble on his ear and a tongue massage down to his dick, he felt different. He couldn't think of the last time he and his wife had sex like that.

Love, Fire & Ice

****

Dexter was on his way to Vegas for another visit and he couldn't wait to see Vanity. He had called her several times but the call was going directly to her voicemail. The few days leading up to the trip, he noticed their talks were shorter and shorter. He could not land fast enough before he gave her a call again, right from the tarmac.

What Dexter didn't know was that Winston had planned a surprise getaway for Vanity. Winston booked the trip just after their rekindling rendezvous a few days earlier. It was to the place they honeymooned nearly twenty years ago. That morning, Vanity got ready for work; she came down to the kitchen and prepared to leave, and noticed that Winston was still there.

"You're running late, aren't you?" she asked.

"Actually, I've taken the day off so I'm going to take you to work today," he said.

"Excuse me? Did you say a day off? Did the school burn down?" she said sarcastically.

"I know. It has been a long time since I have taken time off. I told the Dean that I needed a little time and he just looked at me and laughed. He asked if I was dying or sick with some deadly disease," Winston joked.

"Yea, well, I am right there with him. Come here and let me feel your forehead." Vanity laughed and leaned forward to feel Winston's forehead.

"Oh, that's not necessary. Besides, if you feel on my head, you're going to be late for work," he said.

"Okay, well let's get going, I want to stop at Starbucks."

"You drink that?" asked Winston.

"Yea. Lately, I have not really been in the mood to make coffee in the morning so I've been stopping there." Vanity concluded.

Winston drove to the Starbucks on the corner and went in with Vanity to see what all the fuss was about in that place. He looked at the price for coffee and nearly choked.

"This is what it costs to drink coffee from this place?" he asked flabbergasted.

"Don't make a scene, Winston. It's OK. I've spent way more on worse," Vanity said in a whisper.

Winston felt weird ordering anything from this place but when they got to the cashier, he ordered a banana nut muffin since he had his morning cup of coffee already. After they got the coffee they headed toward the airport which was opposite of where Vanity worked.

"Where are we going?" she asked.

Love, Fire & Ice

"I didn't think we would get too far off course before you noticed that I've kidnapped you," he said.

"Kidnapped me? What do you mean? Where are we going, Winston? I have several meetings this morning and I can't be late," she fussed.

"Mrs. Vanity Davis, please calm down. I have taken care of everything. Just relax and let me do this. Okay?" he concluded.

At that moment, the little light bulb came on in Vanity's head. She did not say another word the entire ride. She let him drive confidently to wherever he was taking her. When they pulled up into the airport, she knew it was a trip. To where, that is what she didn't know. When they received their boarding passes, Vanity was able to see they were going to Miami. She wondered why he chose Miami but didn't ask. She was starting to let things just happen and let Winston do his thing, which so far was feeling good.

She pulled out her phone when they got to the gate and saw that she had several missed calls and two text messages from Dexter. "Oh, no." She thought. Dexter was planning to be in Vegas. Somehow, with all of the attention from Winston, she forgot. It was only a matter of time before this kind of oversight would happen.

She replied to the text message, "Hi. I am traveling unexpectedly. I will call you later. I am at the airport."

Dexter did not respond until it was nearly time to take off which was about an hour later, "When are you coming back?" He asked.

"I don't know. It's a long story and when I get there, I will give you a call. We need to talk," she responded.

Not another word form from Dexter. When a woman says she needed to talk, there was some serious business about to go down and it was usually nothing good. The flight to Miami was easy and Vanity slept most of it. At the Miami International Airport, Winston had arranged for car service.

They made their way to South Beach to find the streets already filled with locals and travelers. The weather was mild and the sky was clear. The sun beamed down on the hotel balcony where they stayed on their honeymoon night. They could see the beach, ships and boats miles and miles out into the ocean. Vanity loved the view and Winston remembered that.

"Are you ready for some lunch, Van?" Winston asked.

"Sure," Vanity said in a dazed whisper.

"Are you okay? You're awfully quiet." He asked coming to her side.

"Yes, I just feel a little tired. Maybe it was the flight," she said.

"Are you sure? We can cancel lunch if you're not up to it."

"No, maybe I need to eat something. Besides, I don't want to ruin your plans."

"Only if you're sure, we'll go. The car is already downstairs waiting for us."

"Let's go." Vanity grabbed her handbag from the chase sofa and started toward the door.

When they made it down to the lobby of the hotel, Winston stopped by the desk to give them the itinerary for the evening. They stepped out of the hotel where they were greeted by a chauffeur and a black Bentley. Vanity had not been in a Bentley in a while and it was quite nice. The leather was soft like butter and it sat up higher than her sports coupe and she liked how that felt. They pulled away from the hotel and people from the streets looked at them trying to see who was inside.

The restaurant was on Ocean Avenue and was in the mix of all the hustle and bustle. Winston had made reservations at the first restaurant they dined at back when they came for their honeymoon. Vanity was shocked that he remembered all the details from so long ago and even more surprised that the place was still in business. The establishment wasn't fancy but she knew it was more about the memory.

"The food is just like I remember," Vanity said.

"Yes, I know. Remember we ate here every day for lunch?" Winston said.

"I do. We were so scared to venture out back then. It looks like they've at least kept the place current." She said looking around.

"Yes, I made sure they had a good rating before I booked it. I would have hated to book it long distance and not know if they still had good service," Winston said.

Winston was always a stickler about that kind of thing. He had to check for ratings and customer service comments online before buying anything. It wasn't a bad thing but sometimes Vanity thought he could be over the top. She was excited that this place passed his test because the food was great.

After lunch, the car picked them up and took them over to Bayside to do some shopping. Every time Vanity came to Miami, she did her souvenir shopping off the beach. She wanted to pick up things early so she would not forget. She went into a store to look at t-shirts for her staff when her phone rang. It was Dexter.

Winston was off in another shop looking at hats so she decided to answer.

"Hello."

"Vanity, what's going on? Why are traveling? You knew I was coming," Dexter questioned.

"It was a trip that was sprung on me by Winston. I couldn't say no," she explained.

"Why not? You're not falling for his stunts to win you back are you? I thought we had something real," he said.

"We do. It's just the way things happened."

"You slept with him didn't you?" He asked, already knowing the answer.

After a moment of silence, "Yes, I did."

"How, when?" Dexter asked with disappointment in his voice.

"He seduced me one night and I couldn't resist."

"Then what?"

"Next thing I knew he had this trip planned to where we honeymooned."

"And where is that?" He asked.

"Miami."

"Miami? Wow. You guys are just rekindling the flame, aren't you?" His disappointment had turned to anger.

"Dexter, please don't be like that. I am not sure what I feel right now. It's just too much going on and really, I needed to get away from Vegas for a few days. It has nothing to do with you but just everything that's going on," she said.

"Honey, is everything OK?" Winston came up behind Vanity with his hand on the small of her back.

Startled by his abrupt approach, "Oh, yes. I was just talking to Cole and letting her know things were fine here, that's all." She didn't give Dexter a chance to say anything before she disconnected the call.

"Are you sure everything is OK? Did I plan this trip at the wrong time?" Winston asked concerned.

"No, it's not that. I just have a lot on my mind. This trip was very much needed." Vanity said with sincerity.

The situation with Dexter after this week was really wearing on her. She was not able to be into both her husband and Dexter. That just wouldn't work.

Ever since the sex they had, Winston had been extra attentive to her and she didn't seem to mind. It was what she wanted, right? That her husband paid her a little attention and that is what he was doing.

After shopping Vanity was exhausted and wanted to head back to the room. The car waited curbside to take them back over to beach. Before they made it to the bridge headed to seaside, Vanity was asleep.

Winston nudged her to wake up, "Honey, wake up. We're at the hotel."

Vanity struggled but she woke up and got out the car. Inside their room, she plopped down on the sofa.

The bellhop brought up their bags and sat them inside the room just behind them.

"I think I need a nap," Vanity finally said.

"Okay. I am going to take a stroll. We do have dinner reservations tonight. Do you think you'll be up to it?" He asked.

"Sure. I just need a little cat nap," she said, yawning.

"I will be back shortly." He said and was gone.

Within moments, Vanity was in dreamland.

****

Back in Vegas, Dexter along with his team met with Cole at the firm. Dexter had to disguise his disappointment and keep his focus on the development of his campaign. He was angry that Vanity had taken off to be with her husband without telling him. He was jealous. Cole noticed Dexter's distractions as she saw him looking out the window a couple times. She knew Vanity was away and based on Winston's calls to her to reschedule all of Vanity's meetings, she was sure that Dexter had no idea she was planning to be away.

After the meeting was over Cole asked to speak to Dexter for a few moments. His partners went out to the lobby to wait. Cole said she would stay out of it but she was going to find out what had him so distracted even though she already knew.

"Are you OK, Mr. McKnight?" Cole asked.

"No. I was thrown off my game today. I will be fine." He said.

"Anything I can do?" Cole offered.

"No. We will reconvene in three weeks. I'm sorry for being distracted. Thankfully my team was here to pick up the slack." Dexter confessed.

"Okay. We will see you all in three weeks. Please stop by Michelle's desk and she will schedule the meeting," Cole said.

Cole got up from the conference table and extended a hand for a shake. The two departed the conference room and Dexter stopped to join his team. Cole said her goodbyes to them as she headed toward her office. Cole wanted to call Vanity to find out what she told Dexter because he was extremely unfocused on business, which was not a good thing. She warned Vanity that business could be at risk if things got messy. Cole thought of making the call and decided not to get involved. She just prayed their affair would fade into the closet of memories for both Van and VanCole.

****

Vanity woke up to the sound of Winston coming back it to the room. She looked at the alarm clock next to the bed and realized that she had been sleep for over three hours. The late afternoon sun was shining bright in the window of their suite. When the sun was ready to set, she would have a perfect view. Winston had made plans for dinner but Vanity was fine just staying in the room. She had picked up a novel from the airport for the flight and had yet to crack the cover on it.

"Hey sleepy head," Winston said.

"Hey." Vanity said in a still sleepy voice.

"Are you up to going out for dinner?" Winston said hopefully.

As much as she wanted to say no, "Yes. Let me get dressed." Vanity looked around the room for her luggage but realized that she did not pack anything.

"Did you pack my things?" She thought about how horrible her wardrobe would be if he did but she was hopeful.

"Actually, I have your wardrobe arriving any moment." A knock on the door took Winston away from the room to let the bellman in. He rolled in a cart with garment bags from C. Madeline's.

"Oh, my goodness." Vanity saw the bellman take the garment bags and hang them in the closet. Winston gave him a tip and he left the room.

"What is all of this?"

"I didn't bring any dinner attire for you so I went out today and picked out a few things, with the help of some fashion experts at the boutique." Winston said.

"What did you get?" Vanity hopped up from the sofa and went to the closet to peek at the clothes. When she unzipped the first bag, the most stunning black Ceil Chapman vintage dress spilled from it. Vanity covered her mouth in amazement.

"Winston, this is..."

Winston came up from behind and hugged his wife as she admired the dress.

"Let's shower and get dressed for dinner." He said as he took his wife by the hand and led her to the master bath. He allowed Vanity to shower as he laid out another lingerie set he purchased from her favorite boutique along with the shoes the boutique had helped him select for the dress, a pair of open toed lace heels with diamond studs along the strap. He was proud of his choices, especially the vintage diamond necklace to compliment the dress. In all of their years of marriage, he had never spent this much money at one time on his wife but he felt like he would give up everything at this point to save his marriage.

Vanity made her way out of the shower just as Winston jumped in. Vanity was in total awe. She did not know who this man was but it wasn't her Winston. He had never done any of these things for her and for this to be happening all of a sudden, and all at one time; she didn't know what to think. She didn't want to get suspicious that this was all a set up to win her back from her "supposed affair". Was he turning a new leaf and these were the things he was going to start doing to keep their marriage exciting? Either way, they were working because she felt pampered and showered like a woman likes to feel from time to time. She took her time putting on her body oil. Winston had brought her regular essentials from the house including one of her favorite perfumes. When putting on the dress Winston came out of the shower just in time to zip it up.

"It looks stunning on you," he said with kisses to the back of her neck, "and you smell good, too."

"Thank you." Vanity ran her hands down her body, as she looked in the mirror and saw that the A-line dress did everything right to make her curves sexy. She sat on the bed to put on the shoes that made the dress sexier on her. She felt like Cinderella getting ready for a Ball. Winston came from the bathroom in his tuxedo; he looked as handsome as ever. Vanity couldn't remember the last time they went to an event together that required this much attention.

"Now this is the man I married," Vanity said as she went to her husband and grabbed his bowtie and straightened it up for him. Winston took his wife by the waist and brought her to him for a kiss. It was deep and sensual. Their tongues played gently with each other and from their closeness Vanity could feel his nature rising and her pussy moistening with each tongue thrust.

Vanity unbuckled the belt to his pants and freed his manhood. He was ready and so was she.

She didn't care about the reservations, the dress or the shoes she had on. She wanted some of her husband right now! When she hiked up the fluffy dress to expose the panties, Winston gave her ass a smack that excited her to no end. She leaned on the dresser drawer and spread apart her legs giving access through the peek a boo panties for Winston to slide his dick right in. His pants down to his ankles he made his way inside his wife's juicy pussy. Although it appeared like a quickie, he took his time as he enjoyed the fantastic view in the mirror of her breast protruding from the strapless dress; he looked down at the diamond-studded heels that made her legs long and sexy. He kept the strokes nice and slow to keep the sweat to a minimum. His hands on her waist, he brought her to him, he tapped her ass again, and she moaned, "oooooh, yessss..." Vanity took him in and matched him to get her own enjoyment. She took all he was giving and with each tap of her g-spot, she knew her climax wasn't far. He felt her muscles tighten and her moans, "oooh, yea! Shit...I'm coming!" got louder. He fucked her harder and harder at the sound of her screams, and within seconds, their orgasms competed for oxygen as they spilled from her pussy to the floor.

"Babe, that was awesome." He said tapping her on the ass one last time. They went to the bathroom for a quick wash up as if nothing happened.

Vanity applied her makeup and was almost ready to go when Winston came up from behind. He admired his wife in the mirror.

"Something's missing," he said.

"What?" Vanity asked.

She had her diamond-studded earrings on from her own collection but her neck was a little bare, so Winston must have forgotten her jewelry.

"Close your eyes," he said.

She did. When she opened them, he had placed the most exquisite diamonds around her neck. Her eyes began to swell up in tears.

"Please don't cry." Winston asked of her.

"I can't help it."

"Why? You don't like it?" He asked.

"I love it and I love you, Winston." Vanity finally confessed.

"I love you too, Vanity and I always have. I would never do anything to hurt you. You know that," he said.

Instantly Vanity felt sick to her stomach. So nauseous that she ran to the bathroom and threw up. Winston ran in behind her.

"Are you okay?" He asked patting her on the back.

"Yes. I think it was something in the food this morning." Vanity said, embarrassed by the incident.

On their way out to dinner Vanity thought that Winston outdone himself. They dined at a five star restaurant on Ocean Avenue and had the best time. Vanity was getting looks all night from the women in the restaurant looking at her vintage dress and necklace. She definitely felt like Cinderella.

When they got back to the room that night, Winston rubbed her feet and made her some hot tea to help her stomach settle down for the night. It was the perfect night. What Vanity had been missing in her husband had come through all in one night. He was attentive, spontaneous, and thoughtful and was able to please her sexually.

Six

Ever since that first night in Miami, Vanity had been getting nauseous and queasy. It was starting to get annoying, especially when she would throw up in the middle of the day. Cole noticed it immediately on Vanity's first day back at the office.

"What's up with you? Are you sick? Are you coming down with something?" She asked.

"I feel fine. I think I need to change my diet or something. Fried foods just aren't agreeing with me," Vanity said.

"Well don't be here spreading your germs if you are sick. Those stomach viruses or whatever it could be are contagious," Cole said.

"Yes, I know. What's up with the McKnight deal? How was their visit?" Vanity switched the topic to business.

"It was fine except the fact that Dexter was so distracted during the presentation. What's going on with you two? Did you end it?" Cole asked.

"No, I have not officially ended it but I plan to this today. Winston did more than enough for me to feel like we still have a chance," Vanity said with a smile.

"Do share," Cole said.

Vanity shared all the girly details of the trip to Miami. Cole couldn't wait to see the dress, shoes and necklace that Vanity raved about. Cole was smiling and happy that her friend had found peace in her marriage and had not completely given up on it. After their chat, Vanity called Dexter to have the "we need to talk" conversation.

"Hello," Dexter said.

"Hi. It's me Vanity."

"Yes, I know. How are you?" He asked.

"I am doing fine. We need to talk," she said.

"I know what you're going to say Vanity. No need to get all sentimental," he said.

"I'm sorry but I had to give him a chance. He wasn't ready to give up on us like I was," she finished.

"Is that right? So where does that leave us Vanity?" He asked still hopeful.

"Dexter, please do not make me choose. You know what's right," Vanity said.

"Do I?" He said.

"You should. I mean, look at us. We are married people with lives that affect other people; we can't dismantle our marriages just like that. We have businesses, people who depend on us for their livelihoods. We cannot be that selfish," Vanity explained.

"You've obviously given this some thought. You make me want to keep doing all of that, Vanity. I am not ready to give that up, yet." He said.

"We don't have a choice, Dexter."

"What do you mean by that?"

"It's over. We have to end this before our families end up hurt behind our selfishness," Vanity said.

"Over? No, not over the phone, not like this. I want to see you." He demanded.

"I don't think seeing each other will change anything Dexter. Its best that next time we see each other that we are focused on your project and getting your operation here up and running," Vanity insisted.

"Oh, so we're all business now, is that it?" Dexter was growing angry.

"I do not want us to be at odds but we were taking a risk in the beginning and if we want this to end without everyone finding out this is the best," she said.

"I am taking the next flight out." He said and hung up the phone.

"Dexter..." Vanity said but he had hung up. She did not try to call him back because she knew he was serious and would be in Vegas in a few hours.

Vanity had to prepare herself for this confrontation and get it over with. She had no idea how to convince him after the way he reacted but she had to try. It was hard for Vanity to focus on the rest of her day, not knowing when Dexter would be arriving. He was taking a chance leaving home and coming right back to Vegas after just leaving. What would his wife think? Vanity started to feel weak in the stomach just thinking about it.

"Cole." Vanity pressed the intercom to her partner's office.

"Yes. What's up?" She answered.

"Please come over," Vanity said.

Moments later Cole was in Vanity's office and from the way Vanity looked, something was definitely wrong.

"What's wrong Van?" Cole asked.

"Dexter. He's on his way back to Vegas," Vanity said.

"But why? He just left. What did you tell him?" Cole said.

"I tried to tell him that Winston and I are going work things out but he wanted to come here and have this discussion in person. What is he thinking coming back to Vegas?" Vanity said.

"I told you this could end badly." Cole said shaking her head.

"Please, don't give me that I told you so speech. I need to end this calmly so Winston doesn't find out. There isn't any proof that I've actually cheated on him. And I want to keep it that way." Vanity said.

"Well, I don't have any advice for you. I cannot believe you have put yourself and this firm in this mess. As your friend, I'm disappointed and as your partner, you need to fix this, quietly," Cole said obviously upset.

"Thanks for your support." Vanity said sarcastically before she turned her attention to her beeping cell phone.

"Is that him?" Cole asked.

"No, it's Winston. He said dinner tonight at Caesars." Vanity said.

"I hope you don't cancel on him to meet with Dexter." Cole spat.

"I don't intend to cancel on Winston. He's been doing everything right and I do not want to give him any reason to think something else is keeping me from him." Vanity said.

"Good. I will help you this one time so when Dexter arrives, just direct him back to the office and I'll stick around until you and Winston finish dinner. I will call and ask you to meet me here for a last minute meeting so you can end this." Cole suggested.

"Thanks. I owe you, sis." Vanity said.

"Yea, well you are my best friend so I want to see you come out of this all right, even if that means I have to step in." Cole said.

Just as they suspected Dexter arrived as soon as Vanity and Winston ordered their food. Vanity sent Dexter a text telling him to meet her at the office and that Cole would be there to let him in until she got there. Once he arrived, Cole gave Vanity the call that she needed to come back to the office before heading home. That was Vanity's cue to let Winston know she had to go back to the office.

"Do you want me to hang out with you?" He offered.

"No, it's probably a presentation she has for tomorrow that she needs my help on, it can take a minute or an hour and I know you have class in the morning. I'll be fine." Vanity assured him.

"Okay. Well if you change your mind, let me know," he said.

After a nice dinner at Caesars, they parted ways. It had been years since they met for dinner after work. Vanity had started making dinner plans alone. When she got home most nights Winston was already in bed or had eaten without her.

Love, Fire & Ice

The ride back to the office was too short for Vanity to get her thoughts together. She tried to think her way through this situation during dinner but she didn't want to seem preoccupied without alarming Winston that something was wrong.

When she arrived at the office, she saw a few employees' cars and the rented Porsche Dexter drove when he came to Vegas. She took a deep breath before going into the office for the confrontation, for a face-to-face end to their affair.

Vanity came off the elevator, and Dexter was waiting in the lobby. Agitation was written all over his face, one for waiting on Vanity for nearly an hour and two for having to come to Vegas to deal with this. He stood to greet her when she exited the elevator.

"Hello, Vanity." He said sternly.

"Hello, Dexter. Let's go to my office." Vanity said as she didn't pause for a hug or even lose a beat in her stride toward her office. When she closed the door, Dexter grabbed her hand gently and pulled her close to him. Vanity couldn't help but respond to his emotions. She couldn't be mad or even put up a fight. She still loved this man and he knew it by the way she let him take her into his embrace without saying a word. His cologne was intoxicating and when he took a nibble on her ear, she melted inside.

"Dexter..." She tried to stop him.

"Wait, Vanity before you say anything, let me have you one more time before it's over. I could not let you end this over the phone. I needed to see you, be near you, and touch you." He said with his hands caressing her backside.

"But Dexter..." She tried to say but his lips found hers and the words from Vanity faded. His tongue got deeper and deeper with each thrust, the teasing became more and more sensual and before she knew it, Dexter was up her blouse and under her bra. Her nipples were erect and ready; they recognized his touch, his energy. It wasn't supposed to happen like this but she didn't stop him.

He guided her to the sofa, his mind made up; he wasn't going down without a fight either. Why? She didn't know, but he was determined to satisfy her right then and she wasn't stopping him.

The skirt that Vanity wore that day made it easy for Dexter to gain access to her wetness. He spread her thighs only to see her sexy lace panties already giving him access to her. His tongue went straight for it and soft moans came from Vanity. She grabbed his head when he hit the right spot on her clit, and because he stayed on it, she came profusely. Dexter gave her that look that he wanted to join in her pleasure. Positioned on his knees, he pulled her toward him and thrust into her in the same move. It was forceful, with anger and passion, she could not tell which emotion over ruled the other. He wrapped her legs around his waist and went in as deep as he could.   He had every inch of himself inside her, and stroked hard as he kept his inches firmly planted in her throbbing wet pussy.   It was almost violent sex, but she enjoyed. He was scratching a wall in her pussy that sent fire through her blood, he stared in her eyes with a passion that held Van in suspense until they both came and this time Vanity let out a little squeal that could have caused alarm but no one came knocking.

Their breathing, hard and labored, came to a normal pace before either of them started talking. He was still on his knees when he laid his head on her stomach.

"I'm in love with you Vanity. I want to see more and do more with you. I did not want this to end, not like this, not so soon," he said.

"I didn't expect this either. I'm confused, Dexter. I love you but I love my husband too. How do I do this?" Vanity said.

"I can't make you choose me over your husband, but I would like us to keep our special bond. You've awaken things in me that has been dormant for years and I want that to continue," he said.

Vanity said, "I think we both did that for each other but how do we do this without hurting others and eventually ourselves."

"I don't want you to decide on our future right now, let's not decide this right now. Let's just see what happens. I want to keep seeing you when I come to town and if I can't whisk you away on a lavish trip and shower you with gifts, and then I have to live with that for now."

"I think..." Vanity tried to finish but she felt vomit coming up and she knocked Dexter over trying to make it to the bathroom in her office. She closed the door and stayed in there for nearly ten minutes. The dinner that she just had was gone, just like that.

"Are you OK?" Dexter finally came tapping on the door after fixing his clothes just in case anyone came in. There was no answer but he could hear her sniffling.

"I'll be right out." She managed to say.

By the time she came out of the bathroom, Dexter was sitting on the sofa. Vanity crying, he stood up, "Baby, what's wrong?"

She could barely get it out, "The last time I threw up this much was nineteen years ago when I was pregnant with Christina," she said.

Dexter stepped back and plopped down on the sofa. Not the reaction she was looking for, but at least he didn't ask whose it was.

"How far along do you think?"

"I don't know. We've been seeing each other for over two months and because my cycle is so irregular, I didn't think anything of it."

"Well before you get too upset, go see your doctor." He said.

"You're right. But I'm never sick and this has been my life the past few days." She said.

"Oh, just a few days, it could be anything." Dexter was hopeful.

Even though he didn't say anything, the last thing he needed was a baby from another woman. He loved Vanity, but this was a little much to take on. He thought she was on some kind of birth control, because he never used a condom. Vanity did not know what to think about this new feeling in her. She was sure of what she felt was the beginning stages of pregnancy, but he was right, she should go see her doctor before concluding that she had ruined her life, and everyone around her by getting pregnant by a married man.

Before their conversation ended, Dexter was acting a little less enthusiastic then before. Maybe the news about him having a baby dampened the love mood. Either way, Vanity noticed it.

Dexter had his return flight booked for the last one leaving Vegas. Although he still had a few hours, he was ready to head to the airport. The goodbye was awkward and uncomfortable for Vanity. She didn't know what to think about his mood change.

When Cole came over to see how things went, she knew by the look on Vanity's face that something did not go well.

"Why were you crying?" she asked.

"Something's wrong, Cole."

"What? What the hell did he do?"

"It's nothing like that," Vanity assured her.

"Then what is it?" Cole insisted.

"I think I am pregnant," Vanity said and the tears started to fall.

"What?" Cole yelled.

"Please, keep your voice down and don't sound like that," Vanity said.

"What the hell do you mean, don't sound like that? It's Dexter's isn't it?" Cole assumed.

"Yes, Winston and I just starting having sex last week. It's no way it's his," she said.

"Okay. Sit down. Are you sure you are pregnant?" Cole asked.

Love, Fire & Ice

"I haven't taken a test but like I told Dexter, the last time I felt like this was when I was pregnant with Christina. I am sure. I am going to make an appointment with my OB tomorrow," she said.

"We'll get through this together. Now isn't the time for me to be upset with you. You're already emotional and if you are pregnant, I don't want to be the one causing you any stress," Cole said.

Vanity left the office shortly after meeting with Cole and she had a long, emotional ride home. The things she had on her mind now were compounding fear, anger and love, all as one emotion, tears. She asked herself how in the world she could hide this. There was no way. She had to come clean with her affair or get an abortion. The thought of both made her stomach cringe. Winston would definitely leave her and if she got an abortion to cover up the lie, she would never forgive herself.

****

At the doctor's office the next day, Vanity received confirmation that she was indeed pregnant and based on the timeline she was nearly ten weeks. She couldn't believe that the birth control didn't work. What an affair she thought. It was supposed to be fun, discrete and definitely go undetected; this was not supposed to happen. By the time she made it to the car she was in tears and angry. Mad at herself for being so stupid and even more mad that she was forty and pregnant - a place she said she would never be. She finally built up the energy to pull out of the doctor's office parking lot and head to the office. On the way, she called Dexter to give him the news.

"Hello, Vanity," he answered.

"I'm pregnant," she announced.

There was an awkward silence on the phone before he finally said anything, "What do you want to do?"

"I have not decided but I know it's yours if you had any doubt," she said.

"I didn't," he assured.

"I know if I keep the baby that this will mean we come clean to our spouses about the affair. And if I don't keep the baby, I know I'll never forgive myself," Vanity explained.

"I think that you should take some time to consider what's at stake. I am equally at fault and I will support whatever you decide to do. Just know if you do keep the baby, that this is going to devastate both our families," he said.

"Don't you think I know that?" Vanity grew agitated.

"Calm down. I do not want to make you upset. I just want you to know that it can be stressful on you and the baby," he said.

Vanity did not know one way or another, what his intentions were at this point, but she was done with the conversation. She could tell that he cared about the situation, but she didn't know if he was still looking out for himself and making sure that his wife and family did not have to be exposed to such an affair.

When she got back to the office, she told Cole what the doctor said. They both were not as happy as one should be with such news but Cole didn't judge her friend. She wanted to be by her side because she was definitely going to need it.

The rest of the afternoon was a blur. The meetings she had, she put off on her other associates. She was distracted and could not focus on any presentations at this point. It took all the energy that she had to conduct a tele-conference with an overseas client that she could not cancel or pass on to anyone. After that meeting, she wrapped up and headed home.

In the garage, Vanity contemplated telling Winston but then figured, it was still early on and it could just be a waste of time telling him anything but she knew deep down that she had to confess the truth. It was going to devastate him; especially after all he did in the last week to make things better.

When she came through the kitchen, she saw Winston reaching in the oven. He turned to greet his wife and saw that she looked like she had been through the ringer. "What's wrong?" He said as he pulled the oven mitten off his hand.

"Sit down, Winston. I need to talk to you," Vanity managed to say.

"What is it honey? What's going on?" He said as he grabbed the chair at the kitchen table.

"I am pregnant," she blurted.

"Pregnant?" At first, his expression was excited but then he thought for a second and the smile dissipated and turned into and angry scow.

"What do you mean you're pregnant? It's impossible for us to be pregnant," he said.

"I know, Winston. The baby isn't yours," she said and closed her eyes.

There was dead silence in the room and from the way, the chair hit the floor Vanity knew that Winston had pushed back from the table and left the room. Her eyes closed she feared what he would do but she could not face him. She hurt her husband of nearly twenty years with not only an affair, but also a baby that wasn't his.

Winston left the kitchen, and he did not return. The meal he was preparing was left unattended; he didn't care. Vanity turned off the oven, wrapped up the food and went to bed.

Vanity tried to get out of bed the next day but couldn't manage. She called Cole to let her know that she would need a few days to sort things out, get her head together. Winston had packed some bags and left the night before without a single word. She thought he would blow up and fuss about this, but he didn't, and that scared her more. She did not know where he went and he had left his cell phone. He was gone and she had no way to contact him.

Seven

Spring break was here and Christina was expected to come home for about a week. Vanity had no intentions on telling her what was going on. It had been weeks and Winston had not come home or called. She had hoped he realized that his daughter would be home and he would at least come and see her.

The all-day sickness was still in full force and Vanity was in the bathroom throwing up after every meal. She tried every trick in the book to get over it but the little bugger would not quit. In a sick kind of way, Vanity felt it was Karma smacking her in the face for having an affair in the first place. Cole had come by every day to keep her company since Winston left. Vanity had decided to keep the baby now that Winston knew about it. Dexter had not told his family yet, but she didn't care. He still wanted to be part of the baby's life but he felt he was not ready to tell his wife yet.

Dexter was also due in Vegas for the next baby checkup. Vanity felt bad having him around, but she needed support and she didn't want to go through this pregnancy alone. Winston made it perfectly clear that he wanted no part of it and who could blame him? That still left Vanity alone; she welcomed Dexter to be there for her. The times that Vanity lay alone in her bed she thought about what in the world, she would do with a newborn. She had yet to get excited about the baby. She feared she would be a bad mother, too involved with her career, now possibly single, with no husband or full time support system. The thoughts made her feel like an immature teenager who got pregnant on her first time around. She had no answers.

At the doctor's appointment, Vanity and Dexter would hear the baby's heartbeat. Dexter who has three children of his own was not new to this but for some reason he felt like Vanity and this baby were different.

"Wow. Listen to that" He said putting his hand over her belly.

The nurse moved the monitor around and did it a few more times. It sounded like irregular beats but she said, "Sounds like there are two in there."

"Two? Two, what?" Vanity asked.

"Two beats. We'll need to get an ultrasound to be sure but I've been at this for over thirty years and I know two heartbeats when I hear them." The nurse assured them.

"Oh, my goodness." Vanity laid her head back, with hands over her face, she could not move. Karma was a bitch she thought. She was having twins. This was much worse than she thought. How in the hell did she plan to take care of twins by herself? She wasn't superwoman, nor was she prepared for all that diaper changing, potty training, and first day of school crap that came with this territory.

"Don't worry yourself, Van. We'll get through this?" Dexter said.

"We? I am doing this alone! You are married. My husband left me!" Vanity replied, with attitude.

The nurse quietly cleaned off the machine and gave them time alone as she went to get the ultrasound machine.

"Winston left?" Dexter asked.

"Yes. He left the night I told him. I haven't seen or heard from him since. I've been alone." Vanity said sadly.

"Why didn't you tell me?"

"What were you going to do? Leave your wife to come here to be with me?"

"At least I could have made arrangements to come in to see you more often than just for the appointment." He said.

"You know, this is just a mess. What was I thinking? I should have never slept with you!"

"Do you regret what we have?"

"You mean, had?"

"Had? What are you saying, Vanity?"

"I don't know what to feel about this anymore."

The nurse tapped on the door and came back into the room with the ultrasound machine. She put the ultrasound jelly on her stomach and confirmed two little babies growing inside Vanity. She gave Vanity the black and white snapshot of two little growing babies. The nurse grabbed the chart and made her notations.

After the nurse wrapped up the doctor came in to do his five-minute chat and was gone. Dexter and Vanity went to the parking lot to talk before he headed back to the airport.

"Can I at least hire someone to come and clean and cook for you?" He offered.

"Dexter, that isn't necessary. I can manage. Besides, Cole has come over everyday.

"Are you sure?" He confirmed.

"Yes, I will be fine, now get out of here so you can catch your flight." Vanity leaned in for a hug and Dexter responded with a sensual peck on her soft lips.

Even though this situation was starting to feel awkward it felt good to get the kiss and feel wanted by

Dexter knowing what was about to come. Vanity did not mention it, but she was going to the airport herself to pick up Christina.

Christina's flight was due in about thirty minutes so Vanity had just enough time to drive over and wait for her to come to the curb. When she arrived at the airport, Christina was already at the curb waiting. Her flight must have come in a few minutes early. Vanity pulled up and popped the trunk.

"Hi mom!" Christina said when she flopped down in the passenger's seat.

"Hi baby. How was your flight? "Vanity asked.

"It was fine. I couldn't wait to get here; my friends are planning some cool parties this week during spring break," Chris explained.

"Well, I guess you'll find some time to spend with me. Let me know in advance so I can keep my schedule open." Vanity said.

On the ride, back to the house Christina told her mom about her grades, and the opportunity she has to go to China with one of her classes. Vanity was anxious to hear about the details and told Christina that it was an opportunity that she shouldn't pass up.

"Is dad home?" Christina asked.

"I'm not sure. I haven't talked to him today. I know they are on spring break also this week. He might be. We'll see when we get there." Vanity said.

When Vanity pulled into the driveway, she did not see his car but when she opened the garage, she saw his car parked in its normal spot. A sigh of relief came over her because she didn't have to explain to her daughter what they were going through; at least not today. Winston came from the house to greet his daughter.

"Hi, sugar bear." He came over to her side of the car to open the door.

"Hi, daddy," Christina said.

Vanity popped the trunk and struggled to grab the bags but Winston came over and assisted her, "I got it." He said avoiding eye contact with Vanity.

"Thank you." She said but he was already walking away.

"So, sugar bear, how is school." Winston said once they made it to the kitchen.

Christina told her father the same story she told her mom about grades and traveling. He agreed that she should plan to go.

"What's for lunch? I'm starving. Let's go get seafood!" Christina was excited to be home.

"I guess we better go because once you start hanging out with your friends, we're going to be lowest on the totem pole." Vanity said.

"That's right, dad. So, let's go." Christina insisted.

****

The restaurant was not crowded this time of day so they could be seated immediately. Vanity looked at the menu and tried to find something that wouldn't make her sick but it was going to be a gamble and the last thing she wanted to do was get sick in front her daughter.

"I'm really not hungry right now, sweetie. I'll just eat some of the bread they bring out but you go ahead and get what you want. I want to hear more about school." Vanity said.

Winston gave her a funny look. This was also Vanity's favorite place to eat seafood and for her to skip it meant that she probably would get sick eating it. He recalled when she was pregnant with Christina how she couldn't keep anything down. The bread she said she would eat, probably not a good idea either, especially with all the butter they put on it. Christina excused herself to go to the restroom and Winston broke the ice between him and his wife.

"How are you?" He asked.

"I am not okay but I will manage." Vanity said.

"Who's the father? Is it that man I saw you with?" He asked.

"Yes. I lied to you and this is what I get for it." She answered.

"You know I do not wish any ill will on you, that is not who I am, but I have to think about myself right now. I cannot go through this with you. I cannot be a part of this pregnancy and raise another man's child." He explained.

"Children." Vanity clarified.

"Children? What do you mean children?" He said confused.

Vanity felt like it was no sense in keeping any details away from him, "Its twins."

"Twins?" He said in shock, "What the hell are you going to do with twins? Is this man going to help you raise them because I sure as hell want no part of this?"

"Winston, please. I do not expect you to do anything. I am keeping them and will do the best I can." Vanity said.

"Good. I have taken some time to think about this and I'm moving out of the house." He said.

Vanity wasn't surprised to hear him actually say it but deep down she was still hurt and felt more alone than ever. Her eyes started to fill and she tried to wipe them away before Christina came back to the table.

"I understand and we better tell Chris so she knows what's going on. She's not a kid anymore." Vanity said.

"I am not telling her, you are." He said.

"Fine." Vanity said and excused herself from the table.

"Where's mom?" Christina asked when she came back to the table.

"She'll be right back. So, what are you going to order?" Winston asked looking at the menu.

"I think I want the ultimate feast." Christina said.

"Me, too."

Vanity came back in and slipped into the restroom to freshen her makeup to cover any evidence of crying. She couldn't be upset with Winston, he was the victim in all of this and she understood if he didn't want to be around her.

After they had lunch, they headed back to the house. Christina was texting her friends for their first meet up. When they arrived Christina's BFF was already there waiting. She left her parent's car and went to hang out with her friends. Winston and Vanity were alone again.

"Are you moving out while Chris is here?" Vanity asked as she put her purse down on the table.

"No, I have to make some permanent arrangements but it will be as soon as she heads back to school." He said.

"Winston, I am sorry for what's happened. Things were looking much better before this and I hope one day you can forgive me." Vanity said.

"Are you still seeing him? You know what, never mind that, Vanity, I really thought we had a chance to fix whatever was going on with you and your feelings, but apparently, you were well taken care of by someone else. I am sure I can forgive you someday, but today is not that day, I just can't." He said and walked out of the kitchen to the staircase that led to the master bedroom.

Vanity went into the den, and found a comfortable spot on the sofa. She drifted off into a deep sleep. Something she had been doing a lot of lately since she had been home alone. To stay busy she had cleaned up every room in the house and had reorganized her closet and hired a crew to handle some other odd things that she and Winston had put off for some time.

****

Halfway into the pregnancy, Dexter and Vanity began seeing each other weekly. Dexter put Vegas on his weekly itinerary for business purposes to make sure Vanity did not go through this experience alone.

Winston moved across town, closer to the university. Christina called her mother everyday instead of emailing to check on her. Christina was not as disappointed as Vanity thought. She knew her parents were rocky and she couldn't be mad at her mother for being pregnant. She offered to move back home to see about her but Vanity wouldn't hear of that.

At the next doctor's appointment, they were to find out the sex of the babies. Dexter planned to meet her at the office on his way from the airport, and then to VanCole for a meeting right after. When she arrived at the doctor's office, she signed in, but waited for Dexter to arrive before seeing the doctor. She looked at all the other soon to be mothers and she realized how different she was from them or at least appeared. She was a married woman with a married man's child. That alone bothered her, sometimes unnerved her security of self. When Dexter came through the door, looking like GQ, all of the women looked at him with a double take; Vanity couldn't help but smile as she temporarily forgot about how wrong all of this was.

Hell, she fell in love with a married man who just happened to be so damn sexy, all the time. He leaned down to kiss her on the top of her head before sitting down next to her.

"Hi, babe," he said.

"Hi. How was your flight?" She asked.

"It was fine. How are you feeling? Are the babies fighting today?" He asked. During their frequent talks, Vanity would tell him about the kicking on both sides of her ribs.

"They've been pretty calm today," she said.

"How about the morning sickness, is that still getting better?" He asked.

"Yes, I think these rascals are finally settling in," she said.

The nurse poked her head out from behind the door and motioned for Vanity and Dexter to come back. Inside the ultrasound room, Vanity and Dexter awaited the announcement of the sexes of their twins. The same nurse who gave them the twin news was conducting the ultrasound. Vanity got undressed and into the gown and with Dexter's help made her way up on the table. The nurse placed gel on her belly and turned on the machine.

"Okay, looks like this one over here," she said pointing at the monitor, "is a girl. And this one over here is..." She moved the wand around trying to get the best look "is a boy." She pointed at the little penis standing at attention.

"A boy and girl?" Vanity repeated.

"Yes, now this is not 100% so don't go out and paint one room pink and one room blue." The nurse said with a chuckle.

"Of course." Vanity said without a smile.

Dexter had not spoken a word yet.

"Are you okay, Dexter?" Vanity finally asked.

"Uh, yea. Reality is really setting in. We are really going to do this," he said.

"Setting in? Ahhh, it's been set in, right in my belly that is getting bigger by the day, or haven't you noticed?" Vanity was confused and annoyed by what he said.

"Yes, I've noticed. I didn't mean anything by it. Let's just finish the appointment. Don't you still need to see the doctor?" Dexter asked.

"Yes," the nurse interjected and following Dexter's lead to deflect from Vanity's apparent annoyance.

"Okay, then let's get through this. I don't want you getting upset," he said.

"It's too late but I will not press. Okay, nurse, tell the doc I'm ready. I have a meeting to get to."

Vanity and Dexter made it back to the office at the same time. He was on the phone when they arrived so he motioned to Vanity that he would be a few minutes. When Vanity made it to her office, she had a few minutes to do some things before the meeting. With

Vanity obviously showing, the office staff made special trips to see her. Cole knew about the appointment today to find out the sex so as soon as Vanity sat down she got a call.

"Were you watching me come in?" Vanity said, laughing.

"You sound like you're in a good mood. I'll be right over." Cole said.

When Cole went to her partner's office, she got the news about the sex of the twins. Cole was very excited and gave her best friend a hug.

"Cole, I'm even more scared. What am I going to do with twins?" Vanity said to her friend.

"You're going to be just as great as you were with Christina." She assured her.

A tap on the door, Michelle poked her head in. "Ms. Davis, the sheriff is here to see you."

Her heart dropped, thinking something happened to Christina. She made her way out to the lobby and the sheriff walked up to her, "Mrs. Vanity Davis?"

"Yes." She answered.

"You've just been served." He handed Vanity a manila envelope.

She stood in the lobby dumbfounded. It could only be divorce papers from Winston. When the elevator opened for the sheriff to get on, Dexter was exiting. He saw the flushed look in Vanity's face.

"Is everything OK?" He asked looking back at the sheriff who disappeared when the elevator doors closed.

Vanity didn't say anything; she turned to walk back to her office. Cole was right behind her and so was Dexter but before he could cross the threshold, Cole stopped him.

"Do you mind waiting out in the lobby for a minute. I'll let Michelle know when it's okay for you to come in." She didn't wait for a response before she closed the door in his face. She joined her friend at her desk as she saw her opening the envelope.

"Is it that what I think it is?" Cole asked.

Vanity looked at the first page and it was divorce papers from Winston's lawyer.

"Yes." Vanity answered as she flipped through the papers to see the reason. He stated irreconcilable differences, which was strange since that was not the obvious reason, but she guessed he had his own face to save.

"Vanity, I will have Michelle contact your lawyer." Cole offered.

"No, don't. I do not want my business floating around the office any more then it is. I know people are talking about the pregnancy, so I will handle this privately." Vanity said.

"Dexter is waiting. Do you want to have the meeting with him or do you want me to do it?" Cole asked.

"Go ahead. I need to start making some calls. I have to stay focused and stress free. I think I need to work from home for a few weeks until I can get things in order. Are you OK with that?" Vanity asked.

"Of course, I can handle things around here. Do you want to talk to Dexter before the meeting, he's waiting outside?" Cole asked.

"Yes, send him in. Afterwards, I'm going to leave and go see my attorney." Vanity said.

When Cole opened the door, Dexter stood up from the chair in the lobby. She gave him the nod to go ahead in, "After you see Vanity, you can meet me in Conference Room B." She instructed.

He went into Vanity's office and closed the door. "What's wrong Vanity? Why was that sheriff here?" He asked.

"This." She handed him the envelope. He read the contents and sat down on the sofa. He put his head down and couldn't speak a word except, "I'm sorry."

Vanity did not respond right away. She took out her phone and made a call to her attorney for a walk-in appointment. When she hung up the phone, she looked over at Dexter and smiled, "Don't be sorry. In hindsight, I was asking for this by getting involved with you. These twins did not create this problem. I just didn't have the courage to end my marriage the right way." Vanity said.

Surprisingly, she was not upset about the divorce papers. She knew they would come, she just thought he would wait until the babies were born but the inevitable had arrived. Vanity explained that she would not be attending the meeting and would be taking a few weeks off from the office. Dexter agreed that she should take it easy; she was halfway through the pregnancy and did not need any stress. Vanity packed up her things and left for her appointment.

At the attorney's office, Vanity asked her to explain what Winston was requesting as far as the settlement. The only thing he asked for was the rental properties they owned outside of Vegas. He didn't want her money or anything from the home they shared. He was angry but he wasn't that guy. He did not want to uproot Vanity or expect her to find a new home in her condition. It looked like a pretty cut and dry divorce so her attorney recommended Vanity to sign them so they could be filed for a court date. She advised it could take up to sixty days before getting into court. However, because it was going to be an uncontested matter, she might be able to get things done on an expedited basis to minimize any stress Van might experience. Vanity thought about that timeframe and knew she'd be big and pregnant by then. "Please do what you can as soon as you can. I really don't want to roll into court. I need to keep this as private and quiet as possible."

Eight

The closer Vanity came to the due date of her twins, the more she feared facing reality. She wanted to love the idea of being a mother again but the feeling was just not like it should be. The situation they were being born into just wasn't right, or fair. She contacted her attorney about adoption. She was eight weeks away from the due date, and if she was going to make a decision, she had to make it now.

Vanity had not told Dexter about her thoughts or contemplations. They had a well-baby appointment and she planned to talk with him over lunch afterward. She didn't think he would be upset, especially since he still had not told his wife; which still upset her in a way.

Dexter had flown in the night before because Vanity had an early appointment. He tried to see her but she had become moody and less interested in seeing him since she had gotten so big with the twins.

"Hi, Van," he said when he came through the door into the doctor's office. He was dressed down in a sweat suit and sneakers but still looked like he was from GQ magazine.

"You look beautiful." He kissed her cheek.

She patted her protruding stomach and said, "thanks to these rascals."

"Hey, don't call my babies, rascals," he joked.

The nurse came out and called Vanity to come back to see the doctor. When she got up on the table for her exam, the doctor told her that she had dilated about a half inch.

"It's too early for that, right?" Vanity asked concerned.

"Yes, it's nothing to alarm you too much. I will be putting you on bed rest, though to be on the safe side. We need these babies full term." The doctor ordered.

"Bed rest?" Vanity said disappointed.

"That's right. Do you have someone who can take care of you or do you need to be in the hospital?" The doctor asked.

"Yes," Dexter spoke up quickly, "I'll be taking care of her."

The doctor and Vanity both looked at him, but Vanity's gaze was more from confusion. The doctor smiled and said, "That's the ticket, a strong support system is very important in the last trimester."

Vanity didn't know what he was agreeing to. She could only stare at this man. Dexter stared back into her eyes, but didn't say anything. Vanity was immediately worried about the health of the babies, and wanted to make sure she did everything to ensure they were okay. Dexter's quick emphatic response was surprisingly providing Van with a level of comfort. She had not gotten any form of real emotion from Dexter since she told him of the pregnancy. He had always seemed so in control and unshakeable that she generally felt he was just going through the motions with her.

After the appointment Dexter told Vanity to drive her car home, he wanted to take her somewhere. She agreed and Dexter followed her to the house where she parked her car in the garage. As they drove, Vanity decided to tell Dexter about her doubts, she needed to see his response to what she coined now as "Her decision".

"Dex, I have something to tell you," she started, and then paused, as she looked out the passenger window.

"I am sure if I can keep the babies." She finished.

"What? Why?" He slowed the car down and pulled over to the side of the road. His tone sounded devastated.

"I cannot do this alone. I'm a career woman, which is why I only had one child. I am not ready to start over.

Besides, you are married and you can't be in their lives on a part time basis, and I don't want to raise them living your double life. It's not fair to them or me," she explained.

"Vanity, I'm sorry that you feel that way. I've been here for you as much as I could." He started.

"That's not going to be enough for these twins and you know it." Vanity said matter of fact.

"Vanity, I can't make you change your mind, so of course I will agree. Will you have access to see them?" Dexter knew that she wanted to give the twins up for adoption.

"I don't know. My attorney is writing up the details. I needed to tell you about it so we can sign the papers before you go back to Denver."

"Okay. Whatever you need me to do," he leaned over, grabbed her for a kiss, "I love you so much Vanity." He put their foreheads together for a moment and let out a deep sigh.

"I love you, too." She said.

After realizing she was pregnant, Vanity and Dexter had not had sex, but it was moments like this that gave her heart the pitter pat, and she knew she was still attracted and loved this man.

After their moment of clarity about the twins, Dexter drove off to take Vanity to the surprise he had planned. The business construction, weekly meetings, traveling back and forth, and the hotel expenses were adding up. To minimize expenses and ensure Vanity would be taken care of, Dexter rented a condominium for the next couple of months. He wanted to be around for the last few weeks of the pregnancy just in case Vanity went into labor and he could not get to her in time. Now that she was on bed rest, he could care for her around the clock. He owed her that much.

When they pulled into the community, Vanity recognized it. She knew a few people who lived in the community over the years. It was a trendy young community, but expensive and exclusive. He got out of the car to open her side. They walked up to a door located on the lower level. He opened the front door to reveal a fully furnished contemporary layout.

"Who lives here?" She asked.

"You do for as long as you want," he said, giving her the spare key from his pocket.

"Me? But, why?"

"So I can be here with you until the babies are born."

"But why?" she asked again.

"I told the wife that these last few weeks are very critical to the grand opening and I needed to be here for the next two months. I will go home on the weekends and I figured Cole could stay with you while I'm not here," he said.

"Oh, baby!" Vanity tried hugging him without poking the crap out of him with her stomach. She took an assessment of the condo room by room. When she made it to the master bedroom, she went straight to the oversized bathroom with a matching closet. It was stocked with clothes for a woman and man.

She turned to Dexter "Whose clothes are these in the closet?"

"They're ours, baby."

Vanity felt like a kid in a candy store because Dexter went out of his way to make sure that she felt at home. She went back into the master bedroom and sat in the rocking chair off on the corner. It was the kind made for nursing mothers. Sadly, Vanity did not intend on using it for that purpose but it sure was comfortable and by the end of the night, she was in it relaxing from all of the excitement the day had brought.

The next morning, after an uncomfortable night's sleep, Vanity had a list of things to do before she was stricken to the bed. Dexter overhead the conversations and did not like the idea of Vanity being on her feet all day but he knew that he would not be able to talk her out of it and really, he shouldn't, what right did he have? They both needed to get things in order for the babies as soon as possible. He was trying to wrap his mind around her doubts; he wanted to be okay with it, as Vanity had seemed very acceptant of the idea of other people raising their children. He was not, and doubted that he ever could be.

Up to now, Dexter thought that he and Vanity would be the parents. He hadn't spoken with his wife about the affair, and now that they intended on giving up the children for adoption, it was possible that he could keep his secret forever. Vanity had not spoken to her family in Denver either, they didn't know about the affair or the babies and she planned to keep it that way.

****

After the first week on bed rest, Vanity was going stir-crazy sitting in the house. Dexter had been cooking dinner and handling all of her needs but she needed to get out of the house.

"Baby, I need to get out of the house. Let's go out to eat today."

"Are you sure you should be on your feet?"

"I need some fresh air."

"Okay, but we won't be out long."

"Okay." Vanity agreed.

They made their way to the other side of town for a buffet of a mixture of good and bad foods. Vanity had a very healthy portion of both. She wanted to feed these hungry babies and get some enjoyment out of being able to keep a meal down. Indigestion had been a problem for some time, and had just begun to get better.

On the way to the car, Vanity glanced over to the bookstore across the parking lot and saw Winston walking to his car. She tried to look away, but it was too late. Their eyes connected.

"What's wrong? You haven't said a word since we got in the car.

"I saw Winston a few minutes ago."

"When?"

"When we were leaving the restaurant."

"Oh. He doesn't know I'm here with you does he?"

"No. I literally have not spoken to him in months. It just felt awkward with him seeing us together."

"Yea, well, someone has to be with you. So, let's not focus on that. Remember the doctor said we have to stay positive to keep you and the babies healthy. Any stress you feel will transfer to these innocent babies." He said, as he reached over to rub on her stomach.

"You're right." Vanity said and laid her head back on the headrest.

Her thoughts went to a place they had not since she first announced that she was pregnant. She felt like she and Dexter were a family, it was as if he wanted to be with her and raise their children. Was adoption the right thing to do? Could they be a family one day?

The thoughts were pleasing her soul until a sharp pain from her lower abdomen caused her to scream and open her eyes. Dexter swerved the car to a stop.

"What is it?"

Vanity grabbed her stomach. "I don't know. That was the worst pain I've ever felt in my life!"

"Was it a contraction?"

"I hope not," but no sooner than the words fell out of her mouth, another pain. This time Vanity felt wetness in her clothes. "I think my water just broke."

"It's not time yet." Dexter said in a panic, confused voice.

"I know that! Take me to the hospital!"

"Okay." He said, and drove like a bat out of hell.

Vanity pulled out her cell phone and called Cole. She needed her best friend to be there.

"Hello, Vanity." Cole answered.

"Cole, my water broke."

"What? You're not due yet!" Cole's tone changed to a nervous concern.

"I know. I'm with Dexter on the way to the hospital, just meet us there, please."

"I'm on my way."

Cole was out the office doors within minute. She called Michelle from the car because she wasn't at her desk to tell her what was going on.

Dexter pulled up to the ER and went to get a nurse to come and help Vanity who was starting to have closer contractions. Everything started happening so fast. The nurse immediately took Vanity to the labor and delivery area. Vanity's doctor just happened to be on call at the hospital and came in to give her an exam.

"Yes, Ms. Davis, these youngsters are ready to come on out. Let's get you admitted and prepare you for delivery."

"It's too early." Vanity said, panicked, worried and frightened.

"Yes, ma'am, but you're fully dilated and they're not waiting on your time. You are going into labor; we are going to the deliver right now to make certain no complications will arise for you or these babies, ok? "

Vanity grabbed Dexter's hand and started to cry. At that moment, the doctor's words sank in. Vanity immediately feared for the lives of her babies. They were being born prematurely which meant there were risks and complications that they could have. Within minutes, the room was prepared for giving birth. Cole entered the room with her hospital outfit just in time for the first push. Vanity grabbed both her friend and Dexter's hand while the doctor instructed her to push.

After two long hours and fifteen minutes, the sound of two babies crying filled the room. Vanity was so exhausted that she fell asleep before they brought the babies over. When she woke, her best friend was holding the baby girl and her husband Robert was holding the baby boy.

"Where's Dexter?" Vanity asked first as she cleared her throat.

"He stepped out to take a phone call. He just left." Cole answered as she stood up to hand the baby to Vanity.

"No, not right now." Vanity did not want to hold the baby. She knew that if she did she would want to keep her. It was a mother thing and she knew it.

"Do you want me to go get Dex?" Cole offered just as he came in the room.

"Is everything alright?" Dexter asked coming to Vanity's bedside.

"Yes, baby. Cole, I wanted to wait for Dexter to tell you."

"Tell me what? What's going on?" Cole asked.

Vanity spoke looking directly at the ceiling first, "I thought we still had a few weeks to iron this out but I wanted to tell you that we decided to give the babies up for adoption," Van, looked at the two of them after her statement raised ears. Tears fell from Cole's eyes.

"What are you saying Van?" Cole asked, as she clutched the child closer to her bosom.

Van smiled at the picture of the four of them, they were the family she wanted her and Dexter to be.

"Would you and Robert like to adopt our twins?" She said as her hand made contact with Dexter.

"I don't know what to say?" Robert said looking down at the new baby boy.

"You two will be great parents," Dexter offered.

"Vanity, of course we will." Cole started to weep as she cradled the baby girl.

"Happy birthday, sis. You thought I forgot, didn't you?" Vanity eyes could no longer fight back the tears, she cried for the joy she saw in her best friend, she cried for the love Cole and Robert held for each other and now shared with her babies, Van cried because she was giving away a part of herself to a friend.

"Give us a moment, guys." Vanity hinted for the men to leave the room.

Robert handed Vanity the baby boy and left the women alone. Vanity and Cole shared a moment in time that would make them bond forever.

"Vanity, I cannot believe you're giving your babies to me and Robert. I don't know what to say."

"You don't have to say anything. You are the sister I never had. In my eyes, this happened to me for you. I could never take on these two." Vanity said snuggling up with the baby boy.

"But, what do we do now?" Cole asked.

"I will have my attorney get the paperwork prepared and we'll go from there. Until we have the papers signed, I still have the final say so, and I say they get to go home with you."

Although the twins were born premature they were born healthy and have shown no signs of complications. The girl reminded Vanity of Christina when she was just born and the baby boy had features from his father Dexter. The two of them brought two gorgeous new lives into the world.

Cole smiled, as she looked down at the baby's glowing face "I'm in love already." Cole said kissing her new baby girl.

"So, the fun part begins." Vanity said.

"What do you mean?" asked Cole.

With a bright smile as she wiped away the tears, Van said, "What do you want to name them?"

"Oh, I don't know. I think we need a couple of days to think about it. I'm sure Robert will want a say so."

"I'm sure he will. I get to be the god mother, right?" Vanity joked.

"Of course you do. And you can come take them off our hands whenever you want." Cole laughed.

"Then it's settled. We need to throw you a baby shower!" Vanity said.

"I guess we do. We do not have anything for these two."

Dexter and Robert rejoined the women in the room after their own man talk. Robert found out that, a big baby shower was coming soon, and that he was back on nursery duty. After the death of Raya, nearly a year ago, they had stopped trying to conceive and had turned the nursery into a guestroom. His mind was already working on redoing the room for his son, building another room with private a bathroom for his daughter.

When the nurses came in to take the babies, Vanity let her know about the adoption and to make sure that Cole was who they gave the babies to first. Cole had no plans on leaving Vanity's bedside now that she had two newborns to look after. She even requested a bed to be setup in the room with Vanity so she could stay with her; actually, she wanted to stay closer to the kids. When it was time to feed the babies, Vanity let Cole and Robert do it.

Dexter was somewhat in a daze for the rest of the day. He held the babies a few times but he wasn't saying much. Inside he still wasn't okay with giving up his children to a couple he didn't know, but there was nothing he could really do. His wife and children awaited him back in Denver. He thought about the prospects of giving up what he had built in Denver to satisfy his need and desire for Vanity.

He also thought about other things, like what he would do with two babies from a woman outside his marriage. What would his partners think? How could he explain himself to his family and their friends? His mind stopped asking questions, as he affirmed mentally, "I wouldn't do anything but cause more drama." He knew the twins were better off with a couple who could give them all of the love and attention they needed and provide a stable environment. Dexter looked at Vanity as she stared at him, he sighed and thought that Van knew what she was doing was right, he just had to accept it.

"Hey, I know you usually say who you want to be the godfather, but I'd like to be a part of their lives somehow." Dexter finally spoke as he held his son.

"Sure, man. We wouldn't have it any other way." Robert assured him.

The conversation between Dexter and Robert on their stroll away from Vanity and Cole appeared to have been a good, honest talk. No matter how these two babies came into this world, neither Robert nor Cole was going to hold it against them by not allowing them to have a place in their lives. After all, two healthy new babies brought into this world needed all of the love and family they could get.

Vanity decided to extend her stay in the hospital to get a few things done. She did not want any more accidents in the baby department, unless it was a miracle and the second son of god was being born. She wanted to get rid of eighteen years of old baby fat, and a tummy tuck. After what she had put her body through these past months, Vanity needed a brand new beginning and she intended to get one.

Nine

Vanity and Cole both took time off after the big transition. Cole took a couple of weeks off and Vanity about a month. Cole mostly rotated with a hired nanny to look after the twins while Vanity's time was spent recovering from the birth and cosmetic surgeries.

When Vanity returned to the office, business was booming. They were in one meeting after another and the McKnight Firm was celebrating their grand opening on the week of Van's return. All of the McKnight principles would be in Vegas along with their families. VanCole received an all office invitation to the ribbon cutting ceremony and evening festivities.

Vanity's feelings were in between about going to the after party. Number one, she was without a date and two she was not ready to see Dexter, but on the other hand, she looked stunning and was ready to show off. Dexter had not seen Vanity since he moved back to Denver over a month ago.

Vanity closed the office with the exception of a few associates who stayed back to work on other major deals so everyone else could go to the celebration.

The chain of restaurants back in Denver was not as upscale as the one in Vegas and Vanity had only visited the site once or twice in the very beginning stages. Her team had worked tirelessly on the marketing campaign and the grand opening. The parking lot was full with guests when Vanity pulled in. The sign read, "St. Christopher's". As she walked through the threshold she was in awe...it was exquisite. The décor was upscale American contemporary, marble floors, crystal chandeliers over the main entrance, white linen clothed seating with high back chairs and a fabulous array of floral arrangements for each setting sprinkled throughout the room.

A cousin to Dexter, also a partner, approached Vanity with a smile and extended hand. Vanity only saw her once at the kick off, "Hi Vanity. You look great, girl!"

"Hi, Tiffany. Thanks." Vanity said as she combed her fingers through her pressed out hair and trying to be modest about the compliment, "This place looks very nice. I am impressed with the décor. Did you have something to do with this?"

"I did, but Mrs. McKnight helped out a lot these last few weeks." Tiffany said looking around the room.

"Well you guys did a bang up job. Where is Dexter?" Vanity asked looking past Tiffany and through the crowd.

"He's over there. He just asked me if you had arrived yet." Tiffany pointed over by the podium set up in the corner of the restaurant.

"Great, I'll head over to say, hello." Vanity said as she walked away.

Vanity wore a suit she picked up from Versace just for the grand opening. A short skirt hugged her hips without being too tight and a three quarter blazer. The pumps matched the blouse perfectly and accessories were simple, yet complimented her suit color well. She looked damn good and made a few heads turn in the office that afternoon.

When Dexter turned from his conversation, he saw Vanity strolling through the crowd, his gaze caught her eyes, he was undressing her mentally, pictured her in panties and bra. Dexter did not realize it, but his staring ended the conversation that he was having, made his audience look, too.

"Hello, Vanity." Dexter said leaning in for a quick hug and excusing himself from his guests without an introduction of Vanity.

"Hi, Dexter. I love what you've done here. I can't wait to taste the food and bring some of my new clients to St. Christopher's."

"Thank you. The team has worked very hard and of course, VanCole has a lot to do with that. So, thanks again."

"No problem. Have you seen Cole around? She should be here." Vanity asked looking around the room.

"No, I haven't. By the way, how is she?" He gave her a look that only she would know what he really meant.

"She is doing fine. They all are doing fine. She may bring them since this is a family function."

"Oh, really?"

"Yes, but don't worry, the nanny will help keep the babies out of the lime light as much as possible, but you know how people are with babies." She said with a smile, "I just hope your wife doesn't see the resemblance." Vanity joked, but was dead serious.

"I know. I will try to keep her away from them."

"You don't have to. They are still so new that it's hard to see things like that."

"No, you haven't seen my other son. They do look alike."

"Oh, no!" Vanity said covering her mouth.

"It's fine. This secret won't last forever and I don't want Cole feeling like she has to tip toe around here because of our secret. So, let us enjoy the night. Agreed?"

"Agreed? On what?" the voice of another woman came up to Dexter's side, sliding her arm in his.

"Oh, dear, this is Ms. Vanity Davis of VanCole Marketing. Vanity, this is my wife Francine," Dexter introduced.

"It's actually, Vanity Rodriguez," Vanity corrected. "It's a pleasure to meet you Mrs. McKnight," extending her hand for a shake.

Vanity immediately noticed the Tiffany earrings that Dexter had purchased as a gift meant for her. They looked good with any outfit and she could use the accent since her fashion style was definitely outdated for such an affair.

"Yes, I've heard so much about you. I love your suit." She complimented; which Vanity felt was a good way of saying, I have my eyes on you - bitch.

"Thank you. Well, Dexter, I will see you in a little while. I'm going to round up my staff for a photo on the red carpet." Vanity said trying to get as far away from Francine as she could.

"Sounds good, let's make sure we get one with Cole before we leave. Are you going to the Imagination later for some partying and gambling fun?" He tried not to sound too hopeful with Francine by his side.

"Yes, I plan to be there. See you in a bit." Vanity said leaving the couple to watch her walk away.

Dexter could not help but watch a little longer then he should have. Vanity had definitely whipped her body into shape. He could not wait to get between those legs again, he thought as he watched her glide across the room. Vanity, knowing that she shouldn't, turned to look back at them as she disappeared in the crowd.

Dexter envisioned her legs hanging over his shoulder as he put his face deep between her thighs. Her ass was tighter, legs firmer and breast perkier. Vanity paid a pretty penny and spent time in the gym to tighten up the rest of it and it was showing. She had a glow to her face and a stride of confidence. She straightened her hair so it looked longer and when she walked, the wind made it bounce with each step. He thought to himself that if she looked like this in her suit, "Damn I can't wait to see how she looks like naked." The surprise of an erection snapped him back into reality. Luckily, Francine did not notice.

The ribbon cutting ceremony went off without a hitch. Cole and the twins went undetected and thankfully, because she enjoyed being out with the kids. Vanity was excited to see her best friend so happy. Being a mother for the first time is special and Vanity was glad for her. Vanity gave Cole something of herself that would link them together forever.

Instead of the glow during pregnancy, Cole exuded an afterglow and she looked great.

"How are my little god babies?" Van asked with the oh-so common baby face and smile.

"Cassidy and Collin are doing just fine. The hungriest babies on the Vegas strip!" Cole joked.

"They look so beautiful, Cole." Vanity said leaning down into the carrier to rub on their fat cheeks.

"Yes, they are. We had pictures taken yesterday. I can't wait until they come back."

"Make sure I get one."   Vanity said.

Cole agreed and starting packing up the babies so she could take them back home to get ready for the evening festivities.

"By the way, Robert decided to stay home with the twins, so I could go with you tonight. He figured you wouldn't have a date." Cole joked.

"Is that so? Well, he's right and thanks girl, because I was not really feeling it by myself and I probably would have been a third wheel hanging under you two anyway."

****

Vanity headed home to unwind before getting dressed for the party. Home was still the condo that she and Dexter had shared. After the birth of the babies and once the restaurant was finished, Dexter moved back to Denver with his family. Vanity started to take a liking to it since it was smaller and still gave her the view of the mountains from the balcony every morning. She went to the house only to check her mail and other things. The thought of putting her house it on the market crossed her mind, since Winston did not want any part of it in the divorce settlement. The sale of the house would give her more than enough to buy the condo.

When she got home, she turned on the television to try to catch a rerun of her favorite show "Scandalous". She kicked her pumps off and was about to unbutton her blazer when the doorbell rang. "Who in the hell is that?" She fussed stopping mid-button. When she looked through the peephole, it was Dexter. The bell rang again. Vanity opened the door and their eyes locked.

"I had to come see you." He said.

"You're crazy for coming here. It's too risky." She replied.

"Francine and my kids are sight-seeing. I told her I had to tend to some business for the event tonight so that gave me some time. Time I want to spend with you. I miss you, Van."

Vanity stepped aside to let Dexter into the condo. He immediately took Vanity into his arms bringing her to him for a passionate kiss. It was as if there was no time between them. She instantly felt his dick stiffen, as her body warmed inside. His hands wondered all over her form, touching, feeling and exploring her. His first thoughts of how tight she was, how firm she had become, were right. She was tighter, her ass was firmer, yet she was still soft and subtle to his touch. Her breasts were definitely lifted and firmer. The pouch she had was flat. He ran his fingers through her straight hair as he inhaled the scent of her spicy perfume. Dexter needed his fingers to explore the newness of this woman. He loved this woman before and his love grew deeper now. Not because of the physical transformation, but because of the time she spent understanding, learning and dedicating herself to something other than work. She was a confident woman now. Vanity didn't need that from him anymore.

He lifted Vanity from her feet and took her to the bed they once shared. She finished unbuttoning her blazer and revealed a soft silk blouse that he lifted over her head exposing her lace bra. She removed her skirt, slowly for his eyes to watch, slowly to reveal her hip cut lace panties that barely covered the prize Dexter wanted. The prize she wanted to give him. They were both in mindless lust, wanting each other, wanting to feed from each other.

"Vanity, you are so beautiful."

She lay there with her eyes closed as he explored her. He released her breast and teased each nipple before kissing down the middle of her stomach to hard abs. He was making his way between her thighs. He could not wait to hear her moan for him as she used to. Vanity ached for his tongue to consume her clit. She released her panties by untying the string that kept them together exposing her clean-shaven pussy. With her legs over his shoulder just as he envisioned, Dexter took Vanity into his mouth, sucking, licking and nibbling on her clit, causing multiple moans, multiple orgasms. Vanity wanted more, but she wanted this moment to last. She pulled Dexter up to her and laid him on his back. It was her turn. Vanity grabbed Dexter's dick and gave him a tongue bath that seemed to never end. She gave him the pleasure of a lifetime. He too moaned and loved every minute of her sucking on his dick, teasing and pleasing it. Before he could climax, Vanity straddled him and kept control of this fuck session. Dexter grabbed her slim waist and assisted her strokes to land just where he needed to get that sound out of her, he wanted to hear her voice call his name, he wanted her to moan and speak in tongues as his dick went deeper into her wet pussy. Time was their enemy, but Dexter lost track of time and could only focus on the wetness and tightness of Vanity's sweet spot. Dexter rolled Van over, stood up on the floor and prepared to take her from behind. He wanted to see the perfect ass she had. He smacked it. He rubbed it. He thrust his dick into her as he spread her checks apart, Vanity loved that sensation, and she loved feeling wide open as he stroked her. He felt her body preparing for an orgasm but he wasn't ready yet. He wanted to cum with her; he wanted to experience the orgasm on his dick as he came deep inside her. Vanity could feel his tension, she wanted to cum, but she wanted to milk Dexter as well. Her yoga exercises would pay dividends right now. As her pussy muscle contracted around Dexter's thick dick, he let out a deep animalistic grunt that gave Van a shiver. Dexter tried to stroke deeper as he held her ass, but Van was in control of this, as she released him at the perfect time, she caught every inch of his dick then rotated her hips, as Dexter was forced to release her ass from his grip. She had him locked in and he loved the feeling. Dexter thought being in a standing position would give him support, but it did not. His legs began to quiver. She could feel his thigh muscles jumping as her ass bounced on him, Dexter's face contoured as Vanity laid forward pushing her ass up higher bending his dick inside her. She remembered this pleasure and instantly soaked Dexter's dick with juice, freeing him from her clutch grip. He now had the opportunity to work the head of his dick in that one area, on that spot that made her body spasm, and he did.   Vanity was coming hard, so hard Dexter balls were dripping from her juice. He felt this and immediately began to nut in her. This is what he wanted to feel. He wanted both of them to reach climax together. This was the loving he missed and had to have in his life. Breathing hard, sweat dripping off both of them, Dexter gasped for a word and finally exclaimed, "I don't know if I can ever give you up." He said.

"Is that so?" Vanity said after catching her breath.

"When you're in my world, everything is all right." He confessed.

"Really?" Vanity sounded a little nonchalant.

"You don't believe me?"

"I hear what you're saying but Dexter, come on. We are still just having sex. We cannot have a relationship. This will never be anything more than great fucking."

"What are you saying?" He asked.

"I'm saying that this was a good time but I can't keep doing this with you." Vanity firmly replied.

"Are you ending this?"

"It's been over; I just wanted you one last time for my mental memory. Ahhh, don't you get it?" Vanity was agitated, "You are married. And from the way Francine looks, you're happily married."

"Don't do this." Dexter begged.

"Don't do what? Be honest with myself. I am on the losing end here. I have lost my marriage, given away two beautiful children all because of sex, with you. You haven't given up anything." Vanity said with an attitude that made Dexter realize she was right about everything.

"What do you want me to do? There is nothing you tell me to do that I won't do." He said, as his plea began to sound like that of a twenty-something man that just got pussy whipped.

"I want you to make it right. Be with me or leave me alone." She got up from the bed and pranced to the entryway of the bathroom. Turning around, still naked for him to view her entire body, she said, "Dexter, you can either love me and be with me, or find your way out the door and my life." She went into the bathroom and left him with those last words. She knew he had feelings for her but she was not going to keep the affair going. He had to make a choice. By the time Vanity came out of the shower, Dexter was gone.

****

Vanity had to pick up Cole to go to the party. Since she had the twins, Cole traded in her little sedan for an SUV and that would not be a good look showing up to a party on the strip. When Cole got in the car, she could feel the vibe.

"What's up?" She said.

"It's Dexter. He came by."

"What? What for? Isn't his wife in town?"

"Yes, but apparently she was busy with the kids so he came over."

"Why are you so upset about it though?"

"We had sex, probably the best we ever had, and afterward I told him to choose between me and his wife."

"What? How could you do that? He has kids."

"And? We made two more because of this and besides that he can't keep coming to my bed and having me so caught up into him and then he can go back, have his cake, and eat it too. I can't do that anymore Cole, I can't accept being second to anyone."

"What did he say?" Cole asked.

"Nothing. I left the room to take a shower and when I came back he was gone."

"It sounds like he made his choice." Cole said.

"That's exactly what I said. But, I've decided that I'm going to go to this party, enjoy myself and move on with my life." Vanity exclaimed.

"That's a good idea. Have you seen Winston?" Cole asked changing the subject.

"No. I have not seen Winston since the divorce was final. Other than when Christina is home, we probably won't speak much."

"He called Robert today to ask him if he wanted some tickets to a fight next week. Robert told him sure. He needs a little break from the twins. Winston didn't know you gave them up for adoption."

"Yea, I haven't told him anything about anything."

"I see. Well, I thought he knew."

Vanity changed the subject again to tell Cole about selling the house. She did not want to talk about Winston or Dexter anymore. She had to focus on getting her life back. Business was good and she felt great. The last thing she needed was to keep looking back on should've, could've, would've and a wish.

****

Inside the party, the host who took them to their table. Other staff from VanCole had already arrived. Before sitting down Vanity went to the ladies room.

Standing at the basin, she looked at herself in the mirror. She looked gorgeous on the outside; she wore a simple black strapless dress with the stunning necklace that Winston bought her. Her makeup was flawless and even though her hair was sweated out with Dexter during their overdue sex session, she managed to whip it back into shape. How beautiful she looked on the outside had nothing to do with the emptiness she felt on the inside.

She had no intentions of breaking down, but being with Dexter today did not make things any better. Trying to hold it together, she took her compact from her clutch and patted her cheeks and nose to absorb the annoying shine. In mid-pat, Francine exited the stall behind her.

"Ms. Rodriguez, is it?" She asked washing her hands before taking out her own compact.

"Yes, Mrs. McKnight, but please call me Vanity." Vanity took a quick assessment of her attire and it was definitely a step up from earlier.

"So, you and my husband have gotten rather close during this venture? He's usually not this involved."

"Yes, I would say so. But the projects I work on do require more hands-on to ensure we get the job done." She answered with a sense of sarcasm, definitely pun intended.

"Is that so?" Francine said, poking her lips out to reapply her lipstick.

Vanity could sense the undertone but she didn't plan on commenting on that, "I'll see you around, Mrs. McKnight."

Vanity had already finished primping and she left the restroom before Francine could say anything else. When she made it back to the table, Cole and her staff were laughing and already enjoying themselves. Vanity joined them with all the gumption and bravado she had in her.

After a couple drinks, Vanity was a little looser and felt like she could get on with the night and not be distracted by Dexter, whom she had not seen since she arrived over an hour ago.

"Have you seen Dexter?" Vanity asked Cole.

"I don't think so. I've been here at the table since we got here." Cole replied.

"He should be here by now. I saw his wife in the bathroom when I arrived." Van said with a measure of disgust.

"Oh, did you? That must have been awkward."

"Very!" Vanity slurred.

"Forget about him girl. Enjoy the party, the free drinks remember? Let's order another round."

Cole waved for the server to bring another round to the table.

"You're right." Vanity said finishing off her drink and slamming the glass on the table.

Her favorite song came on and she grabbed one of the guys from her staff to go out to the dance floor. It had been years since Vanity danced at a party like this. It felt like the old club days before she got married. She was not trying to break a sweat but it felt good to get out there. She was determined to do more of that, but Vanity's thoughts quickly went back to her real life. Being single was not all it was cracked up to be.

As she headed back to the table from the dance floor, she looked around the party still trying to pinpoint Dexter. He was still nowhere in sight. Vanity started to get worried. Dexter had left her condo in plenty of time to get back to the hotel and down to the party. Had something happened? She perused around the other parts of the party, but did not see him. She did see Francine again and although everything in her said don't ask, she could not help herself.

"Francine, I haven't seen Dexter. Is he here?"

"Ms. Rodriguez, my husband is fine. He will be here."

"I just thought he'd be here by now."

"Why are you so concerned?"

"Excuse me?" Vanity said offended.

"You heard me." Francine was feeling the liquor and had obviously loosened her tongue.

"This is his party and he should be here that's all." Vanity said.

"You should know, right? I know he was with you before he came here. Yes, I know about you two."

Vanity's eyes opened wider in shock at what Francine had said. How did she find out? Vanity sure as hell did not plan to admit to anything based on that.

"What are you talking about, Mrs. McKnight?"

"Don't fucking Mrs. McKnight me. You've been sleeping with my husband and he knows that I know about it. That's why he's not here."

"Excuse me, I've got to go." Vanity walked away from Francine who had obviously found out something. Vanity wasn't going to stand there dumbfounded. She made her way out of the party and into the hotel's main casino. She found a bathroom and went into a stall to call Dexter. She got no answer. She called Cole to give her a heads up about what just happened and she told her to meet her in the lobby. Vanity wasn't comfortable staying for the rest of the party without knowing what was going on with Dexter and Francine.

After Vanity dropped off Cole, she tried calling Dexter several times. There was still no answer on his cell phone. She called the hotel and got one of her contacts to ring the room number, still, there was no answer. When she got into the condo, she started to worry even more. Francine knew about the affair and now Dexter was nowhere to be found. Vanity dug out some paperwork from the deal and found Tiffany's phone number. When she called, Tiffany said that Dexter never showed up to the party, which ended after Mrs. McKnight made an obscene announcement that her husband was cheating on her and was too embarrassed to show his face at his own party.

Vanity was truly disgusted and almost in a nauseating pain. She was glad that she had already left the party when that happened. Now that the secret was out, there was some explaining she would need to do when she got back to the office. This was not good, not for her, Cole and especially not for the business.

People were going to start putting together the affair and the pregnancy and the fact that the twins are now with Cole. There was nothing she could do about the past but she damn sure wasn't going to sit back and watch her future fall apart.

Ten

There was something wrong with Dexter not being reachable. Vanity would try to call him a few more times before she took a ride over to the hotel. An hour, then two went by, her patience was running thin and without further thought or question, she drove to the hotel. When she arrived, Dexter's rented Porsche was clearly visible to Van, which was not there when she left earlier. As she entered the lobby, Francine was standing at the guest counter.

"Where is Dexter?" Vanity asked in a demanding and angry tone.

Francine obviously drunk or on something, was speaking to the concierge, and glanced at Vanity through blood shoot eyes as she slurred out a reply, "What business is it of yours? Oh, excuse me; I guess he is your business," she said angrily.

"Look, Francine, I don't know what you're talking about but I just haven't heard from him and I'm a little worried something has happened."

Love, Fire & Ice

Francine went from anger to fury, "Look, bitch, you have ruined my marriage and that coward of a man you want wasn't man enough to tell me, so I had to get it out of him myself!"

"What have you done?"

"Oh, I haven't done anything. He just had an accident, maybe. I will tell you what, he's going to pay for what he's put me through. You think he is such a good, caring and loving man. You don't know anything about him. You only know what he tells you. All the good sex, yea, I know he's the shit in bed! I have been with this man for many years and I know he has secrets and you're just another one of his secrets! He's put me through hell over these past years supporting him, his business and raising these kids and this is the thanks I get! Bitch, you haven't heard the last of me either!" Francine said as she rushed away brushing Vanity on the shoulder.

"Wait!" Vanity tried to call after her but Francine kept walking toward the exit with her bags in tow.

The kids were sitting in the waiting area, starring at Vanity as Francine yelled for them to come on, "Let's get the hell out of here."

A yellow cab was waiting in the galley just outside the hotel. Vanity turned to the concierge and asked for the McKnight room number. She had that kind of pull at the Imagination and this was the perfect time to use it.

She took the elevator to the twenty-second floor and made her way to the room. At the room 2218, she knocked and received no response; she could not hear a sound emanating from behind the doors. Vanity was not sure what Francine meant when she said, "He had an accident, maybe."

Vanity was scared now; she felt terror in the pit of her stomach. She was worried that he could be hurt badly and left alone in the room. Vanity knocked again and still no answer. Thinking quickly, she went back down to the desk and explained the situation. The night manager came out to assist and when he heard the story, he authorized the entrance into the room. Technically, Francine checked out, so the hotel staff could go in, but Vanity did not want to wait for housekeeping the next morning to find Dexter in a state far past help.

When they opened the door, Vanity rushed in to search the room, but no one was there. Where was Dexter? Francine was gone and Dexter was nowhere in sight. Arriving back in the lobby, Vanity contemplated calling the police to report him missing but as soon as she pulled out her cell phone, she heard a voice call her name, "Van." The voice was weak but she recognized it.

It was Dexter. She turned to see him coming in the main entrance. His clothing was torn, his face was badly beaten and he still had on his tuxedo.

"Dexter!"

Vanity ran over to him and tried to hug him but his body crumbled to the ground, "Call 9-1-1!" Vanity screamed, as she fell to the floor with him in her arms.

When the paramedics arrived, everything happened so fast. Van heard them say things like possible internal bleeding as one heavy deep cough caused blood to gush from Dexter's mouth. It was a daze of words, feelings and emotions for Vanity. By the time, he was on the gurney; she was in her car ready to follow the ambulance through the city.

The racing thoughts came under control as the silent ride gave her a moment to gather herself for whatever would happen next. He would need her to be strong for him, she told herself. Vanity also needed to think about how this could have happened, all of it. How did Francine learn about them? Who attacked Dexter and why? What would happen next, was she next?

The ambulance ahead of her screeched to a halt in the emergency room entrance. Vanity found a parking space and made her way into the ER. She looked frantically around for Dexter and the paramedics, but neither were in sight.

The nurse seated behind the counter didn't look up or pay any attention to what was going on in front of her, let alone notice the panic and worry on Vanity's face. Vanity tapped on the counter, "Excuse me but a man was just brought in..."

The nurse did not allow another word to come to out of Vanity's mouth before she rudely interrupted her, "Are you the spouse, relative or next of kin?" as she slapped the clipboard on the counter.

Vanity nodded and took the clipboard. Staring at the paperwork presented to her, she was lost and had no idea what to write, what information to put on the forms. Her fingers felt numb and her mind raced to the myriad of questions asked on the forms. As she held the papers before her, a doctor appeared looking around the waiting room as if he wanted to call a name. Vanity saw the look on his face, jumped up and asked the doctor, "Are you looking for someone connected to the man they just brought in?"

The doctor replied, "Yes, are you his wife?"

Vanity responded with a lie, "Yes, I am. What's going on? Where is he?"

The young doctor said, "I'm an intern and was asked to come out and let you know that he is in surgery. I don't have all the details but just as soon as he's stable, he will be out to speak with you. Until then, bring that clipboard with you to the inside waiting room, it's a little nicer and more private."

Shaking her head, Vanity followed the young intern through the doors that the nurse buzzed open. He showed her the waiting room.

As he prepared to walk away, he asked, "Oh, ma'am, what's your name?"

Vanity, looked up and replied, "Mrs. McKnight."

He smiled, nodded his head and walked away.

In the waiting room, she looked at the clipboard still with all its blank spaces and realized she was alone again to face whatever news might be coming through the steel doors before her.

Vanity called Cole, "Hey Cole."

"What's up?" She said groggily, obviously sleeping.

"I'm sorry, didn't mean to wake you up."

Cole replied with a yawn, "I must have dozed off. The twins just went back to sleep. What's up?"

"It's Dexter. Something's happened."

"What do you mean?" Cole asked, now alert.

"He's been beaten badly. I'm at the hospital."

"Oh my god. What happened?"

"I don't know. I haven't been able to find out anything yet. He's in surgery."

"Have you called the police?"

"No. Cole, I don't know what happened. I am not sure if I should."

"Wait a second. Is his wife there with you?"

"No." Vanity told Cole about the outburst at the event from Francine that Dexter was having an affair, and their confrontation in the hotel lobby when she went back to look for Dexter.

"So she's on her way back to Denver? Do you think she had someone rough him up?" Cole asked.

"Rough him up? Cole, he is in surgery. They tried to kill him and they just walked away like it wasn't nothing."

"Vanity you be careful. Whatever she did to him, had done to him, it may also be taken out on you."

"I know. The way she acted at the hotel just seemed a little weird. She looked like an angry woman and you know how dangerous that can be."

"Exactly. Do you need me to come up there?"

"No, I'll be fine. Get some rest. As soon as I hear something I'll let you know."

Vanity called Tiffany and found out that the rest of the firm was still at the hotel. Their schedule had them in Vegas for the first week of the grand opening. No one had any idea what happened to Dexter. Once Tiffany informed the partners, surely they would be on their way to the hospital.

Love, Fire & Ice

****

By the time, they arrived at the hospital the nurse had come out to let them know that Dexter was out of surgery and was stabilized for the moment, but remained in the ICU. The nurse explained that if he had not made it to the hospital when he did, he would have died.

The doctor finally came out, "Mrs. McKnight," as he approached the only woman in the room, "Your husband has a badly lacerated right lung and a collapsed left lung. Four of his ribs are broken, along with the orbital socket of his left eye. We did all we could to minimize the internal bleeding, however, he is on a breathing machine due to the issues with his lungs. Unfortunately, we had to remove his spleen and a section of his liver due to massive trauma."

Vanity's knees became weak as one of the partners noticed the unsteady look of her; he grabbed her arm just as she was falling back. He aided her to a seat as the other two partners were stunned and frozen into place by the doctor's report.

The doctor asked, "Are you alright?" He shined a light into Vanity's eyes.

"Yes, yes I'm ok. I just got a little light headed."

"I'll have one of the nurses bring you back to a room and give you a quick look over, this is a traumatic event and I understand. However, Mrs. McKnight, you must be aware that your husband's condition, his not taken him out of the woods. The next twenty-four hours are critical." He said.

When the doctor left them to get back to his patients the partners stood there in disbelief about what they just heard, Dexter may not make it. He could die.

The nurse came to tend to Vanity, but she refused.

Quietly, Vanity said, "Francine did this."

"Francine?" one of his partners heard her.

"Yes," she told them about the confrontation in the lobby of the hotel. "Francine told me that she knew about the affair and that she was tired of Dexter's lies. She said that she had taken care of him. I didn't know what she meant until he came stumbling into the hotel nearly dead."

As Tiffany entered the waiting room, she heard Vanity's conversation with the McKnight partners.

"Oh, no." Tiffany said.

"What? Do you know something?" Vanity asked.

"Francine went to meet with some of her cousins earlier today. I thought she was going sightseeing and I wanted to tag along, but she asked me to keep an eye on the kids instead. Her cousins are from this area."

Vanity thought about what Dexter had said earlier. He thought that Francine did go sightseeing but instead she was plotting against Dexter.

"Yea, Dexter had mentioned Francine's thug cousins before. They are bad news." One partner said.

"I have to call the police." Vanity said.

"I wouldn't do that." Another partner spoke in a distinct tone and Vanity did not recognize it.

"But we can't let them get away with this." Vanity angrily replied.

Clayton Taylor, a silent partner who lived in Vegas, and Dexter's former economics professor managed to calm down Vanity and explained that it would make things worse by having the police questioning Francine or her family until we hear from Dexter.

"We need to explore angles and outcomes prior to action, let us ensure you are safe, let us allow them to believe they have won. Vanity you go see about Dex and pray. Our answer will come quicker than you think."

The calm steady timber of his voice, his direct words, somehow scared her, she felt a hidden meaning from them, and she saw a depth of strength in his face that was reminiscent of Dexter. Everyone agreed to keep the status of Dexter a secret. They did not want anyone coming back trying to finish the job.

Vanity sat next to his fragile body. Tubes protruded from his mouth and his nose, a thin plastic drape hung around his bed shielding the external elements from his badly beaten body. The bruises were already turning black, and he wore a bandage around his head, eye and chin.

"Dexter." Vanity whispered.

He did not move. She could only grab the plastic surrounding him, her tears silently fell to the ground, she prayed for this man, prayed that life and love would not be taken from her. Vanity looked around to see if anyone was in the area, she placed her hand under the plastic to Dexter's hand. She prayed more, she thanked god for all that she had, all that she was fortunate enough to share in, and apologized for all the hurt she had caused. Her eyes still closed she felt a squeeze. She opened her eyes and saw that Dexter was looking at her. Her eyes filled again with tears.

"Dexter," Vanity managed to say while covering her mouth, "you're okay now. I'm here."

Dexter was alive and although the tube down his throat obstructed his speech; and all he could do was make a gurgle sound and that was enough for Vanity right now.

****

Love, Fire & Ice

Over the next two days, Dexter's health had made significant improvements. The breathing tube was removed, and although a thin air tube remained through his side directly into his right lung, he was able to speak in short sentences with short breaths. His mind cleared more and more every day.

Dexter told Vanity and Clayton what he could remember. Scant details of the beating flashed across his thoughts, but vivid memories of the occurrence were rapid fire in his mind as he slept. He relived the attack almost completely when his eyes closed.

He was knocked unconscious from behind after he parked in the hotel guest lot, he could hear the laughter as they dragged him, locked him into the trunk of a car. His attackers drove short distances, and repeatedly beat his body until pain became an expectation with every blow. Dexter did not know how long this punishment lasted; he had lost all track of time. He recalled passing out and forced to regain consciousness only to be beaten again, the one constant, he never left the trunk of the car.

Clayton was stoned faced as his listened closely to the details. Vanity got the sense that Clayton understood this type of attack, was somehow familiar with this type of torture.

Clayton asked Dexter, "Do you think that Fran could have set this in motion?"

"Francine!"

Dexter's one good eye opened widely, as the monitors connected to him began to beep louder and the indicators turned red. His blood pressure was rising rapidly. He was angry, enraged as reality dived into conscious thought. As the on duty nurse ran into the room, Clayton eased out.

"What did Fran do?" Dexter exclaimed as the nurse insisted that he calm down or he would suffer a stroke or worse.

Vanity hearing this, begged Dexter to relax. In a voice attempting to be reassuring, but trembling in uncertainty, "Please Dexter, just relax and let this go."

Dexter became immediately aware of Vanity when she grabbed his hand and he saw the pain in her eyes, the worry on her face. Somehow, holding her hand, touching her, seemed to calm him.

The nurse said, "Sir, I know that you have been through a traumatic experience, but if you can't remain calm, we will have to restrict visitation. You're here to recover and besides, the police want to speak with you but they have been instructed that you require at least another day, so for your own sake, rest and heal," she said while staring in the face of "*Mrs. McKnight.*"

Vanity had no response for her, just an empty gaze as the nurse turned her focus to adjusting the instruments connected to Dexter. When she left the room, Vanity finally realized that Clayton was no longer there with them.

Dexter said softly, "Francine is responsible for this. She had me beaten and left for dead by her thug cousins."

"How do you know for sure it was her?" Vanity questioned.

"I remember seeing two of them at a family reunion. She tried to have me killed, Vanity."

"Why?"

"I told her that I wanted a divorce."

"You did what?" Vanity tried to yell and whisper at the same time and looked back at the door to make sure no one heard her.

"After I left the condo, I had made up my mind. You are the love of my life and I've always wanted you. Francine was someone I settled with because we had a child together out of high school. When I finally had you, I did not want to let you go. This past year has been the happiest I have lived in years."

"Why did you wait so long, Dexter?"

"I didn't want to hurt Francine or my kids."

"But she already knew about us. How did she find out?"

"She had received a phone call. Someone told her she needed to wake up, she said. She had me followed. I saw the pictures of us, you pregnant with our twins, everything."

"Who, who could have told her, why would..." As Vanity thoughts answered her own question, "Winston," she said painfully.

When Dexter spoke, he did not acknowledge Vanity's statement. "She got upset when I told her that the pictures made my decision easier, I wanted a divorce."

"Dexter, I can't believe you decided that and did not tell me." Vanity said.

"I knew I was going to see you officially single and would not want to let you go and besides you gave me an ultimatum. I had to tell her. I'm not going to spend the next twenty years unhappy, not when it's you that gives me happiness."

"How do you know they will not come back and finish what they started?" Vanity asked.

"Clayton, he will handle things." Dexter replied as sleep quickly came over him. The nurse must have put a sedative in his IV on her last round. For the next several hours, Dexter would sleep peacefully. Vanity never left his side.

As he slept, Vanity thought about where they were at this point, what she had done to affect the lives of so many people. She thought about how she always tried to maintain control of her environment, but this time the elements consumed her, this man had changed her life forever, she had no control over that.

The sedatives administrated by the nurse gave Dexter a healthy mixture of dead sleep and hunger. As he awoke, he muttered, "Damn, I'm hungry."

Vanity finally had reason to smile as she could hear her mother's voice saying, "When you're sick and sleep, and you wake up hungry, well that means you're on the mend." As she pulled closer to Dexter, Van said, "Lunch time is supposed to be here soon. Is there anything I can do for you while we wait?"

Dexter replied, "Actually, there is."

Dexter told Van to get a notepad from the nurse's station; he needed to tighten up loose ends. He was not planning to go back to Denver, but he needed to make sure that Denver would be the end of all of this drama.

He gave her a few numbers to call and instructions for his partners to function as usual. He did not want a fuss over his recovery or bringing any bad attention to the restaurant. After giving directions to Vanity, he was exhausted and fell into sleep again.

Cole had been bringing fresh clothes for Van because up to now, she refused to leave Dexter's bedside. This day she felt a little more secure about leaving his side, she could go home for a shower and prepare mentally to handle Dexter's affairs to the letter of his instructions.

Vanity waited a few minutes stared at his face, and watched him sleep before she gathered her things and went home. On the way, she felt extra paranoid and constantly peered through the rear view mirror. Vanity felt that someone was watching her, following her. When she arrived at the condo she tried to sleep, but she couldn't. Vanity went to the computer and attempted to find out information on Clayton, and dig up what she could about Francine. She did not want any surprises, and as mysterious as Clayton appeared, a surprise was to be expected.

During the search for Francine McKnight, Vanity found out where they lived in Denver and that she had her own accounting business. She could not understand how she could risk losing all of that by trying to hurt Dexter. Nothing about this situation seemed to add up or make sense. Vanity's investigative skills went into overdrive on the internet. She had discovered a host of people by the name, Clayton Taylor. She narrowed the search down to four in the Vegas area, and none of them seemed to fit the profile of the man she met. On the other hand, Francine McKnight was an open book. Vanity got all she needed to satisfy her appetite.

After the sun peaked over the mountaintops, Vanity showered, dressed and headed back to the hospital. When she arrived, she found that Dexter was not in the same room. Back at the nurses' station, she found out that he was moved to another floor. When she got there Francine sitting by his bedside.

"What are you doing here?" Vanity said making her way to the other side of Dexter's bed.

"What am I doing here? I guess you think that just because your secret is out that I am supposed to just let you come in and take my husband?" Francine sharply replied.

"You're the reason he's in here!" Vanity said through her teeth.

"No, you're the reason he's in here." Francine snapped back.

Vanity came around to the side of the bed and Francine stood in defense, "What the fuck are you talking about? I didn't have him beaten almost to death."

"Is that what you think I did? You think that I would have the father of my children harmed. I have nothing to do with this, I'll take his money, cars and the homes, but I won't kill him."

Vanity was not buying her denial and from her body language, she was not there to help his speedy recovery. Dexter laid in a morphine-induced sleep, unaware of the two women arguing over him. Vanity looked Francine the eyes and said, "I will not do this here. You and I have a time and place, this much I swear to you, and just so you know, every time he kissed you," she paused for the right affect, "You tasted my pussy!"

Vanity walked from the room leaving Francine with a look of disbelief and embarrassment on her face. She had to prove to Francine that she may be the wife with the title, but she was the woman he wanted and sticking the blade deep put Francine in her place.

Vanity made her way to the nurses' station, "Excuse me, when Mr. McKnight wakes up, can you please call me at this number? It's very important I speak with him as soon as he wakes. Can you do that for me?"

The nurse graciously nodded and Van went to another floor to cool off and wait.

Before all of this drama, Saturdays found Van in the gym or on the track, and the adrenaline she felt from arguing with Francine, a run on the treadmill was calling her name, but she knew better, she needed to be close when Dexter woke up. She just could not stay in the same room with Francine. Vanity wondered how she could show her face. How did she even know where he was?

While she waited, Vanity used her time productively, she made more calls to his partners to let them know his instructions, she called his attorney and left a message that it was urgent that he get back with her. Lastly, she called Clayton, "Mr. Taylor?"

"Yes, Vanity?" He replied.

The voice of Clayton Taylor made Vanity nervous, "Francine is in the hospital, she's in Dexter's room, I don't know how she found him, but she's here."

"Hmmm, Vanity have you ever been shark fishing?" He asked.

"What? No, what does…" She started.

"When you hunt shark, you let the monster come to you, that's what we did. We spread out the chum to see which shark will come to feed." Clayton's response sounded simple, yet cold and calculated.

Vanity replied, "What type of game are you playing with Dexter's life Clayton? You've seen what they did to him. This needs to end and I need your help…"

Silence fell on the line. Clayton was no longer there, "Hello?" She looked at the phone in confusion about what was going on. What the hell had Dexter got her mixed up in?

Vanity finally got a call from the nurse's station. Dexter was asking for her. When she got back to the room, Francine was gone.

"Where did your wife go?"

"Fran was here?"

"Yes, and blaming me for putting you in the hospital."

"What? Baby, you know I don't think that. What was she doing here, why is she back in Vegas?" He reached out for Van's hand and he kissed it.

"I don't know but I don't like it. Something is not right about how she is acting."

"What do you mean?"

"I mean she just looks frazzled and her eyes look kind of bugged out like she's just wired up about something."

"Did she say something about the attack?"

"No, but it's written all over her face that she was not happy to see your recovery."

Dexter listened intently to Vanity explain the argument while he was asleep.

"Dexter, I don't know what she has up her sleeve but I'm not going to sit around and not do anything. We have to get the authorities involved, even if just to file a report on the attack."

"You're right. The nurse left the detectives card on the table. Make the call and get them up here to take the report. I remember some details but a lot of it is a blur. I do not even remember how I got out of the trunk, or how I made it back to the hotel. I just remember seeing you standing there and when you came over to me everything went black again."

"Save the details for the police so you only have to say it once. You need your energy, just rest." Vanity called the police.

Before the police got to the hospital, Vanity asked Dexter, "What's the deal with Clayton? He scares me, he is so, shadowish, not at all like an economics professor, and believe me I know professors and he's not one."

Dexter smiled, as he looked out the window, he sighed and responded.

"Clayton Taylor is a former Black Ops Specialist. Oh, and he does a have masters in economics. I've known him for years and he covertly protects my family and me from people that are desperate for my money. Let's just call him a professional guardian."

Vanity was sharp with her reply, "Well where the hell was he while your ass was in a trunk being tortured?"

"He has known about us from the beginning Van. He came to me shortly after we started seeing each and told me I was playing out of my league. He reminded me that Francine had family here and they would have a problem if they found out I was cheating on her."

"That doesn't tell me where he was while they had you?"

"I had him back off so I could come be with you in private, I sent him to cover Francine and the kids," he replied.

"...and that's when she made the switch with Tiffany, she knows about Clayton, doesn't she? She knew he would be on her trail alone, so she had Tiffany take the kids while she made her connections. Clayton could not be in two places at the same time, so he kept his eye on the kids and not Francine. "

Dexter sighed, "Yes...right."

When the police arrived, one of the first questions that he asked was if anyone would want to hurt him. Dexter was hesitant to mention his wife but he had to. With the details that Dexter gave, the detective immediately put out an all-points bulletin for Francine McKnight and her cousins, Tyrone "Cut Boy", Trevone "Hammer" and another cousin only known to Dexter as "Pick".

Vanity sat in the chair next to the bed with her head face down in her hands. She was growing weary listening to the details. All of this criminal activity was new to her. She did not live life like this and she certainly did not fall in love with Dexter to be mixed up in it.

"I don't trust her." Vanity said after the detective left the room.

"She's willing to have you hurt Dexter, possibly killed. I am not sure what she wouldn't do, I'm not even sure what you should do to protect us but I think that we should just get the hell out of here." Vanity was clearly upset. She was panicking. The hot flashes started to come back and her body felt on fire, her mind raced and she was absent of clear thoughts.

Dexter realized what was going on, he saw the confusion and panic in her face. He tried to calm her fears, tried to ease her mind.

"Come here. Let me talk to you for a minute. Don't you know that our life together has purpose? It's you that I love and want. I would give my life to protect you. I'll do anything to protect you in every way. I'm not going to live my life running from her. I'm going to divorce her and move on." He said.

"Will she leave us alone, that's my question?" Vanity still not convinced.

Hesitantly, Dexter replied, "I haven't seen her like this before. She is acting very strange. So, I really don't know. I don't want to put you in the middle of this any further so, I have to put distance between us for a while."

"Yea, well that sounds like a good idea. I think it's time for a trip to Puerto Rico. After the babies and all of this, I need a real break," Vanity said.

"I think that's a good idea. When I get out, I'll have Clayton arrange a place for me to stay; and maybe I can meet you there."

Vanity, looking at the floor said, "Okay. Dexter, I don't know what to say about all of this. Never in a million years would I have thought that we would be here…like this."

"I know honey. Just give me time to make things right."

She could not resist, she had to kiss him, she needed to feel his soft lips, even swollen and bruised, she needed to connect to him, and she needed to feel his energy in her. She had told him before that she loved him, but this time there was a difference, she felt something different.

"Dexter, you're the man I have always dreamed of, you have made me feel a way that no other could, and I will always love you." Vanity said wiping the tears before they fell from her eyes.

Before leaving the room, Dexter gave Vanity information about his plans, but she could not take them in. She began questioning whether her ultimatum was a good idea and if any part of this was her fault. At the threshold of the door, Vanity stopped and looked at him once more and said, "See you soon, right?"

Dexter replied, "It's never too soon to see you, baby."

When she left the hospital, she had no plans on going back. On her way home, she called her travel agent and booked the trip. She had aging grandparents who still lived in Puerto Rico and she had not been in over a year. It was time for a visit. She called Christina to let her know that she would be leaving for a few weeks and to check in with her dad while she was gone. Next, she called Cole to update her and to have her put one of the senior associates in charge of her projects until she got back. Vanity only told Cole a little of the last few events and Cole did not pry; she had enough going on with the twins to be worried about more drama.

At the condominium, Vanity packed her luggage and headed to the airport within the hour. She stopped by the office on the way to pick up a few files so she could monitor a few projects while she was sitting on the beach. When she arrived at the office, there was no one in the building other than the cleaning crew.

"Senora, a package came for you a few minutes ago. I put it on your desk," the janitor said.

"Thank you, Manuel."

When she went into her office, there was a courier package on her desk. She did not recognize the sender but she decided to take it with her and open it on the way. She smiled at the thought that Dexter pulled another one of his gift stunts but she did not have time to wallow in that moment. She had a flight to catch.

After grabbing a few files, she went to the car and tossed the package on the passenger's seat. On the way to the airport she thought about the series of events that was driving her out of the city she loved.

In the parking lot of the airport, Vanity removed the keys from the ignition, laid her head back on the headrest, and took a deep breath. She began to question if this was the right decision, leaving her man, her business. She closed her eyes and dreamed of a new life. The answer came to her, "Puerto Rico bound." Any doubt she had about leaving quickly disappeared. When she opened her eyes, glanced over at the box, she smiled again.

"What has he done now?" She spoke aloud. When she tried to open it, she realized the tape was so tight that she would break a fingernail. The box would have to wait until she got to her gate, she thought. Vanity put the small box on top of the dash so she could grab it after she got her luggage out of the trunk. She pushed the trunk release and stepped out of the car as she was now in a rush. As the keys fell from her hands, Vanity reached down to collect them. Next, a sound unfamiliar to her ears, a sound and force that sent her flying.

"BOOM!"

Epilogue

TWO YEARS LATER

Vanity Rodriguez ~

Sitting at the desk in her office, Vanity turned her chair to look out the window. The sky was reddish-orange and the California skyline glistened as the rest of daylight slowly faded to nights glow. It was something about that time in the day, like in the morning when Vanity found her moments of peace.

After the car bombing Vanity had a lot to be thankful for as she nearly lost her life, eyesight and hearing from the blast. While recovering, she made a pledge to take a moment every day to appreciate the little things, like the setting of the sun.

The scars from the explosion were Vanity's constant reminders that life had its ways of making you atone for wrongs committed. The nightmares and anxiety attacks she experienced after the bombing were other deep reminders, but thankfully, after two years she could finally sleep without aide. Vanity was finally able to get back to doing some of the things she loved and not being afraid to be in public or dreadfully startled by loud noises.

Christina Davis~

Christina graduated from Yale and spent a year in Dubai before beginning her apprenticeship at VanCole. Cole started her from the ground floor. To Christina's credit, she earned her position at the firm regardless of relationship to the owners. She welcomed every grunt assignment Michelle had to offer. She did well. Vanity was proud. Vanity unofficially split her share of the company with her daughter until she felt ready to take it over.

Nicole Daniels~

Cole was deeply in love with family life, the twins and her husband. She viewed Vanity's trials and tribulations from a different window, her view gave foundation to building a loving home.

Michelle Dix~

Michelle became a senior associate, working under Cole. Cole needed someone who could step in immediately when Vanity was out of commission after the accident. Michelle was the one who kept the entire operation afloat and she deserved the promotion with a healthy new salary.

Winston Davis~

Winston relocated to Seattle shortly after receiving a Deanship at the University of Seattle. Leaving his hometown was difficult, but he had to get a fresh start and move on with his life. He needed to find peace with his part in the unfolding tragedy around him. His telling Francine about the affair may have set all of what happened in motion, and Vanity nearly lost her life because of it. The day after the car bombing Winston rushed to the hospital but never made it to Vanity's room. He sat in the parking lot and called Cole for news on Vanity instead. Something inside him would not let him out the car. His own sense of guilt had consumed him.

Two weeks before leaving Vegas, Winston went to see Vanity for the first time since the divorce. Unannounced and unexpected, he rang the bell of home they once shared. Vanity greeted him like a long lost friend, as she felt his pain, and wanted to make amends for her own actions.

Love, Fire & Ice

Francine McKnight & Cousins~

Francine was arrested trying to board a flight to Denver. Her interrogation lasted for two days in connection with Dexter's assault and the car bombing. At the insistence of her attorney, she agreed to cooperate with the local authorities and FBI.

Francine's cousins were eventually taken into custody with the aid of anonymous tips to their locations in various parts of the country. The FBI already had an ongoing investigation into their crime organization "Blood in Blood out" ran by the Bartow brothers, and finally had enough evidence. Apparently, Francine's loyalty to her family had her in business with them. They were all facing charges for money laundering and offshore bank accounts, interstate commerce and countrywide Meth distribution, terrorism and murder. Francine's plea agreement granted her a lighter sentence of fifteen years but her cousins faced life in prison without the possibility of parole.

Dexter McKnight~

In Dexter's the hospital room, the nurse dropped off at his bedside. Just minutes after she left the room, it exploded. Patients in the immediate vicinity were all dismembered. It was a horrible scene.

****

After the trials, Dexter's attorney tracked Vanity down in Puerto Rico and told her that Dexter had changed his will and insurance policies and left everything to her, the twins and his three older children.

The attorney told her, "Quite frankly, it took a long time to inform you because the insurance company refused to budge until after the trial."

Vanity learned that Dexter had multiple insurance policies and the insurance companies had to make sure she was not involved.

Vanity had inherited fifty-one percent of the McKnight restaurant chain, which alone had a net worth in the hundred millions. From that day sitting on the sandy beach, she became a restaurateur whether she wanted to or not.

Losing Dexter and becoming the new owner of restaurants, it took months before she would step foot into her new office but once she did, she did not look back. St Christopher's became the hottest restaurant on the Las Vegas Strip. All ten other locations became upscale including the newest LA location.

Love, Fire & Ice

The bombing had made nationwide news that had opened VanCole and St. Christopher's up to scandal but like all scandals, business did not suffer; they actually gained more customers from all of the publicity.

THREE MORE YEARS LATER

In her Los Angeles office, Vanity was finalizing the details for the grand opening of St. Christopher's in San Francisco, when her assistant walked in.

"The delivery guy just dropped this off for you. It was marked personal and confidential so I didn't open it," she said waiting on Vanity to take the package.

Although Vanity discovered later that the bomb was planted in her car, small packages still gave her a bit of anxiety. Her hand trembled somewhat as she took the package. Her assistant, seeing the nervousness in her face, looked at her puzzled then realized what the look came from, she said, "Ms. Rodriguez, let me open it for you."

At that moment, with those words, Vanity regained composure and said, "No, I got it, thank you Katie, I'll see you in the morning ok."

"Ok, well goodnight and call me if you need anything, I'll be up reviewing the final marketing proposal for San Fran that I got this afternoon from Christina."

Vanity sat in her high back ergonomic chair and stared at the package for a few more seconds after the door closed. She reached for the pearl handled letter opener given to her by the partners of McKnight when she opened operations in Manhattan and D.C. with rousing success over a year ago. The package opened easily, and contained a note and black velvet box. She opened the small box first and yellow canary diamond earrings glistened before her. She read the note:

"Life has purpose."

Her heart skipped a beat and a sigh of relief quietly escaped her lips. She leaned back in the chair, with eyes closed and remembered the love of her life, Dexter McKnight, whom she still missed every day.

The End.

Acknowledgements

To the creator of life, love and happiness, I am thankful for all of which I have the pleasure of enjoying daily.

To my parents, thank you for your support as you give it to me freely and without judgment. You've created a woman of many talents and no matter what I do; you are always there to cheer me to success.

To my daughters (whom I hope won't read this book until they're grown), I love you both and will always support your dreams and nurture your natural talents. Always strive for excellence. Be all you can – as much as you can!

To my friends and family who have ALWAYS supported me! I wish I could list you all by name; but I know I would forget someone so just know that if you're reading these last words, then I'm talking about you! If you know me, then you know my heart. THANK YOU!

About the Author

V. Marie was born and raised in Columbus, Ohio. Pen named V. Marie (Victoria Brock), remembers writing her first book in grade school, titled, "All About Me". The book made with colored paper, affixed by Elmer's® glue, tape, staples and written in pencil, is in a box, still intact as a reminder of how early talents are born. Poems and love letters from high school fill other boxes to support her belief in love and the never-ending possibility of happiness. Who would have ever thought that thirty years later, she would be sharing that talent with the world.

V. Marie hopes you've become a fan *of life for life*. That is the ultimate message. She believes that life is meant to be lived and you will either live it vivaciously – or not and happiness is a state of mind and you will either be it – or not. You choose.

***

If you have enjoyed "Love, Fire & Ice", share your review on the website at LoveFireIce.com.

Book Club Discussion

1. Do the characters seem real and believable? Can you relate to their predicaments? To what extent do they remind you of yourself or someone you know?

2. How do characters change or evolve throughout the course of the story? What events trigger such changes?

3. What emotions (if any) did you feel during the book and at what points during the story?

4. If one (or more) of the characters made a choice that had moral implications, would you have made the same decision? Why? Why not?

5. Did you feel that the book fulfilled your expectations? Were you disappointed?

6. How did the book compare to other books in the same genre?

7. What do you think the main character learned by the end of the book?

8. In what ways do the events in the book reveal evidence of the author's view of life or the world?

9. Did certain parts of the book make you uncomfortable? If so, why did you feel that way? Did this lead to a new understanding or awareness of some aspect of your life you may not have thought about before?

10. Did the book end the way you expected?

V. Marie

Discussion Answers

www.ingramcontent.com/pod-product-compliance
Lightning Source LLC
Chambersburg PA
CBHW021334250626
47155CB00002B/682